INDIAN WINTER

INDIAN WINTER

a novel by

KAZIM ALI

Coach House Books, Toronto

first edition

 Canada Council **Conseil des Arts**
for the Arts **du Canada**

 ONTARIO ARTS COUNCIL
CONSEIL DES ARTS DE L'ONTARIO
an Ontario government agency
un organisme du gouvernement de l'Ontario

Canadä

Published with the generous assistance of the Canada Council for the Arts and
the Ontario Arts Council. Coach House Books also acknowledges the support
of the Government of Canada through the Canada Book Fund.

LIBRARY AND ARCHIVES CANADA CATALOGUING IN PUBLICATION

Title: Indian winter / a novel by Kazim Ali.
Names: Ali, Kazim, author.
Identifiers: Canadiana (print) 20240287258 | Canadiana (ebook) 20240287266
| ISBN 9781552454657 (softcover) | ISBN 9781770567634 (EPUB) | ISBN
9781770567641 (PDF)
Subjects: LCGFT: Novels.
Classification: LCC PS3601.L325 I53 2024 | DDC 813/.6—dc23

Indian Winter is available as an ebook: ISBN 978 1 77056 763 4 (EPUB), 978 1
77056 764 1 (PDF)

Purchase of the print version of this book entitles you to a free digital copy. To
claim your ebook of this title, please email sales@chbooks.com with proof of
purchase. (Coach House Books reserves the right to terminate the free digital
download offer at any time.)

TABLE OF CONTENTS

Chapter 1: Fall   7

Chapter 2: The Photograph   1 5

Chapter 3: Prakriti   2 7

Chapter 4: North Cliff   3 9

Chapter 5: Church Street   7 1

Chapter 6: Volcano   9 1

Chapter 7: Seed Ear   1 13

Chapter 8: Water Sign   1 31

Chapter 9: India Gate   1 45

About the Author   1 57

-1-
FALL

On the way home from the photo shoot, I take a left turn into my drive-way too fast and my scooter skids on the leaves and I fall hard. My helmeted head bangs against the concrete with a smack.

As I fall, I grieve for the body: the weak one, the stupid one that makes always the same mistakes, this one: mine. The neighbour, a young woman – blond and beautiful with a tall and even more beautiful husband, who I always see walking with their two blond and beautiful children – runs over in alarm to check on me. I tell her I am all right, though as I stand, I am dizzy, the weight of the helmet on my head making me feel unbalanced. I insist I am fine. I will be fine.

Though I sway while I am talking to her, and mumble, she determines to believe me and goes back to her children, the beautiful husband perhaps away at work. I watch them walk away on their stroll. Leaving me still standing there, unsteady, trying to maintain my balance.

I spent my morning being photographed in the square, lonely against backdrops of emptiness the photographer chose. A rough oak trunk, a shimmering white wall. The photographer kept requesting that I change looks: an orange T-shirt, a mirrored kurta, a blue blazer, a yellow leather jacket. I made him photograph me wearing the kurta and leather jacket together. Then I insisted he take one full-length, showing that I am wearing the kurta with blue jeans and sneakers. Who am I.

The photographer raved about one particular picture taken against the huge trunk of an old oak, its dramatically ruckled bark contrasting with the deep still and sad look on my face. He says I am beautiful, but more than anything I think I look ravaged, old. It makes me think of the opening of *The Lover*, in which Duras is approached by a man who had known her long before who tells her that he finds her older, aged face more beautiful than her youthful one. In the English translation, by Barbara Bray, the man uses the word *ravaged* to describe Duras's face, but in French the word Duras wrote was *dévasté* – devastated.

I didn't understand until I looked at the picture the photographer was trying to show me. I look vacant, afraid.

Is it true that 'beauty' requires emptiness, a space where nothing exists? That way the viewer can put their own feelings in that place. It's something I'd always believed. But now I think grief is beautiful. A face marked by pain or age. Maybe what people think is beautiful is what is gone? Beauty is death, the void, the forgotten? To be *ravaged* maybe means to be ruined, but to be *devastated* is something else: it means to be affected by life, perhaps profoundly, which is its own kind of heroism.

When I look at the dark space of his camera lens, for the first time I see in my face my father's face. My father, whom I have not spoken to in many years. I left messages for a time. He did not answer. Then when I stopped, he started leaving messages for me. By which time I too found myself not answering. This went on for some time. Until we fell into a pattern of leaving messages for each other. Never suggesting that the other call back, but leaving news: from me, about the garden, about things happening at work, never anything about Ethan, though my father knows he exists. From my father, news about his garden, about happenings with my cousins. I was an only child, a lonely son. Of my mother we do not speak, but on the one-year anniversary of her passing, a package arrived from him, without any note – it had been postmarked the week before, timed so I would get it on the day itself: a watch with a rose-gold linked band and a pale blue face with two butterflies floating on it.

I'm well aware that my mother would not have liked the silence between my father and me, so I prefer to think about the voice mails we keep leaving each other as letters one would have written in a previous age. There are things a human can bear and things they cannot.

I do not like being photographed by someone's phone or digital camera. I prefer the analogue camera. I like the old dark space, the void in the lens, a deep well that could be god or death, just before the shutter opens to see you, to record you, that terrifying moment of annihilation.

—

The memory, Michael, of your fingers on me.
   Will you come?

—

Michael. Who I had neither seen nor heard any news of for many years. I did weep last week when I saw his name in the subject line of an email sent to me by a mutual friend, a woman I knew through Ethan but who had worked with both Michael and Ethan some years before at a bookstore in the East Village in New York. There was no reason on earth for her to be writing me. No reason for her to think I would want news of Michael. Except one reason.

Not often sentimental, I do habitually weep at a particular and peculiar moment: when I move out of a house, I walk through each room to say goodbye. What is it we leave behind? And when we leave this body, this tender one, this stupid one? And how do we bear its pain when it loses other bodies it dumbly loves?

The last time I saw Michael was only a few blocks from that bookstore, at a café around the corner from my little apartment. He has been gone from my life for years. Now he reappears, not just any ghost, but a persistent one.

—

Young gay and trans boys are killing themselves. I start to talk to my friends and family about my own experiences in school. Even my best friend, who knew me more than anyone and from whom I thought I had hidden nothing, said later she had no idea I was being bullied in school. It was silence that kept me in pain, weariness at the fact that no one could see.

Why did I never tell anyone I was being bullied? Not fear that they would hurt me more. No, fear, of course, at that time, of the truth. That what those boys were saying about me was *true*. That I was weak, ugly, a 'fag' or whatever else they called me. Fear that my family would learn why I was being bullied. And that if they found that out, I wouldn't be able to lie. And it took years to know that I never deserved to be treated in such a way and by those very same cruel and beautiful locker-room crushes of mine, their delicate faces and lean bodies that I loved and learned how to love.

Is this why I have always been attracted to men with wounds as deep as my own? When I meet a man who is confident and happy, I normally think of him as a friend. But I could never love a person like him. I mostly loved those who couldn't love me back. Michael.

~

Michael comes, hungry and amiable, to this hunting, my seeking. I hunt and you haunt, or is it me, a mortal revenant, that's haunting you in your spectral life?

~

The trees in fall smell rotten and strange. Broken magnolia flowers litter the sidewalks, and the crushed gingko fruit ice it dangerously. I hadn't cleared the ones in front of the house I shared with Ethan and that is why I skidded on the scooter and fell. By the time he returns home from the day's work on the farm, I have cleared the leaves and the fruit. He does not ask me how my day has gone and I do not tell him that I fell.

~

'How is the book going?' Ethan asks at some point in the evening. We're sitting in the front room, remains of Chinese takeout on the coffee table in front of us. Ethan is reading a book and I am turning tarot cards.

A book? Am I writing a book? Ever since I got Elizabeth's email about Michael, I've been scratching away in a notebook, one of those cheap spiral school notebooks. With a ballpoint pen. Which is how I often write. I don't know why. I suppose it makes it more ordinary. But there's more. If I write longhand, it's more likely I will write short clauses, brief observations, fragments. And writing in such a way appeals to me. A fiction of carefully crafted language with flowing sentences and paragraphs always makes me suspicious. Because it is not how a person's mind works, not really how time works in a person's brain, not really how a person lives their life. At least not for *me*.

I shrug. There's not much point in talking about it. I don't know what the little fragments of observation will make. If it's a book about Michael, there's no plot. Besides, my love affair with Michael, if that's what it could even be called, was over a long time before I met Ethan. Ethan knows him only as a name from the past, someone he worked with briefly at the bookstore but never really knew until he saw me talking to him from across the room at one of Elizabeth's parties. I introduced them out of some perverse belief that the universe might collapse if two men who loved me met each other. But it didn't. Or maybe they didn't love me.

Beneath the nude light of unshuttered street lamps, we sit in silence with each other. I turn another card: the Hanging Man. It's me, suspended there between the future and the past, but suspended too in the present, with Ethan, suspended halfway through a storm-dark day. The street of the city outside is a page, a body, a boundary.

And this? This bending down in front of *why*, this speaking underneath the world: like the basement of the church in the lot next door to the jazz professor's house down the road, which was once the parsonage: when the church was demolished, the basement was sealed off, covered over. The rooms still exist there, his wife tells me, under the sodden green. All the houses beneath the ground we still live in.

And the skin of this, the pulling of threads, mean one might want something to unravel and reveal. *Reveal, reveil, revile, reveille.* 'Can God be approached in language?' asks Christian Wiman. Or do we use the name of 'god' as a gesture toward the place where meaning stops? Declining Gnosticism, Fanny Howe instead says about 'god': 'The longing is the part that's real for me.'

—

'I don't think you should go to India with me,' I say to Ethan. 'There's too much work here.'

He looks at me for a moment; I can't gauge his expression. Then he shrugs his agreement. If he suspects that I'm not being truthful about the reason I don't want to come, he doesn't say anything. He hadn't wanted to come anyway. The farm is a good excuse. Work needs to happen, even in the winter. When did this happen to Ethan and me? When did our lives become ordinary, our love automatic and repetitive, our physical interaction mechanical and uninspired?

—

I'm taking with me the spiral notebook in which I am writing about Michael. Even though Michael is a real person, Ethan believes it is a novel because that is what I have written on its cover. A working title: *Michael: A Novel.*

'He's dead,' I say.

'Who?' Ethan asks.

'Michael. Michael is dead. For years. He's been dead this whole time. Elizabeth only just heard. She hadn't talked to him in a long time either.'

'That's why you've been writing,' he says.

I nod.

Ethan turns back to folding clothes. I honestly do not think he knows who Michael is to me. Was to me. Even though he met him once and knows I am now writing a book bearing his name, he never seems to have figured it out. Even when they met. Even when I held my breath in anticipation of the universe perhaps ending. Which it did not do.

And this life? I am leaving for the winter.

I have to get away from this small Midwestern town and its various dangers: falling on the street, falling into a chasm of loneliness, sitting in a dark house, in silence.

It is not that I will die if I stay here but rather that I am already dead. I am dead and I never had the experience of dying.

And to the dead man comes an invitation to go to India, a series of literary festivals happening one after the other. I tacked on as much free time in between as I could and several more weeks after to stay. Ironic that a dead person must go and then stand in front of people who want – who need – him to be alive.

So I go to India, where both my father and mother grew up – a place where one might dare to be reborn – to write, read, think, all the most important things in the world but which are thought the least important, the most expendable.

-2-
THE PHOTOGRAPH

It is hard to look at the past. Is it a faded photograph you are trying to discern or is it a painting in which reality is manifested by the mind of the artist, the one doing the remembering? Does the one being remembered have any agency to demand being remembered in a certain way or have they, by virtue of being part of history, lost their voice?

In other words, do the dead haunt the one writing or does the one writing haunt the dead, torment one's own past?

I lie on my stomach. Michael's hand on me. The pen gliding across my skin.

Every time I see a person with a tattoo, I think of Michael drawing on my body all the tattoos he wanted me to get.

'But it's permanent,' I say, and he laughs and replies, 'Do you think your body is permanent?'

Though I knew I would never get a tattoo, I let Michael draw on me because I liked taking off my shirt in front of him. I liked his hand on my back. I liked feeling the pen on my skin.

How many years has it been since I'd seen him or even thought of him? We left New York ten years ago, and it had already been years since I'd last seen Michael.

He was the unlikeliest person to have haunted me for so long. He was ordinary-looking, skinny and twitchy. But somehow I couldn't get him out of my mind. The way he turned a pencil in his hands while he was thinking, the way his eyes would drift away from the person who was talking and focus on someone in the distance, a woman arranging a wedding dress in a shop window, or a child walking down the street, licking an ice cream cone.

Any thought of Michael always brings my spring life back to me again, the year I left Albany to move to New York. I was leaving a numbing office job to go back to school. I was turning away from autumn and death and moving into spring. That was the year I decided to dress only in colours of spring: pale green of new leaves, light yellow of the first crocuses, pink of the cherry trees in Washington Park, just outside the window of my apartment in Albany. It was only a year, and then I returned to my habitual browns and blacks and blues, but I felt the colours I wore manifested the changes I was hoping would appear. I was wearing a bright pink T-shirt the night I met Michael, who sported black PVC pants and a silver metallic hoodie, open, with nothing on underneath.

'I think there is no light in the world but the world,' wrote George Oppen. The page is a body to love or maybe a border to cross.

—

I am walking alone, with only the memory of Michael to guide me.
I am lost. Off the trail.
What next.

—

The plane from New York to India is a mythical journey. One goes to sleep over an ocean and then wakes up in a new continent, having lost a day of one's life. Memories of my past lives pass by the present in a blur. Have I brought enough clothes from the last life into this one? India in December is hot, nothing like Ohio, so perhaps I have brought *too* much, am too burdened down by the old memories? Who will I be in a new country?

I do not dare breathe but instead feel myself breathed out by the life I left behind, toward the life in front of me.

December. When I left, ice was dripping from the eaves. Ethan had brought several sprigs of spindly forsythia branches inside to try to force blooms.

Seasons transfer into one another. Time was not on our side.

When I told him not to come, he agreed. Did not insist. He did not want to come. I did not want him to come.

Then I said we should see others since I would be gone for the whole winter. He agreed. I don't know what it means for when I return. I don't know if I care to know.

I don't know if Ethan cares. Or if he cares whether I care. He agreed so easily.

—

Ethan and I met a few years after I knew Michael. It wasn't until Elizabeth's party that I learned they had worked at the same bookstore in the Lower East Side for a little while. He knew Michael at the bookstore, found him as beautiful as I did, but never had the courage to speak to him. Though I didn't learn any of this until after I perversely introduced them to one another. Simultaneously afraid and excited that their meeting might cause the world to combust.

I met Ethan in a yoga class. His mat was next to mine. He was smaller than me, with a haggard face that I would later learn came from long days in the sun due to his work as a gardener. He walks with a slight limp from a childhood injury, but that was something I didn't notice for a long time, and even after I came to know it, sometimes forget about.

We practised yoga next to each other for an hour, and at some point I got wise to the fact that he was peeking over at me as often as I was peeking over at him. The yoga teacher would adjust him and then adjust me next, and I dreamed that it was him touching me. One day, we walked out together and I looked over at him and he looked over at me. We walked straight from the yoga studio to my apartment on 3rd Street without speaking. I opened the door and he followed me inside and we leaned our yoga mats against the wall – carefully, I thought – and then had sex on the floor, just inside the door. It was quick sex, born of long observation and attraction. I fumbled with his belt, immediately sinking to my knees so he knew what I wanted. He slid inside my mouth and then took my head in his hands and pressed himself into me. I relaxed into him so he would know I was his to control. When he was ready to release himself he tried to pull back, but I held him in my mouth and drank him.

We stayed together after that. We didn't talk about it. We didn't label who or what we were to each other. We just kept calling each other, going to the yoga studio, going back to my place. Eventually we were spending all our time together. At some point he moved in.

When Ethan showed me old pictures of himself, I could see how the sun and age had taken his beauty, but I also knew I loved his aged beauty more. Like the man at the beginning of *The Lover*, I prefer his face aged. I prefer it *dévasté*. Ethan has lived.

I didn't think of Michael very much in those early days, except as someone I used to know once, long ago. Someone I had loved a little, or had tried to.

I saw him one single time after the party at which I introduced him to Ethan. He asked me if we could meet, and even though I didn't want to go, I went. As with any old lover, for me the fact of our bodies meeting in physical proximity quivered with weird tension. Is it because I live backward and forward in time at once, I wondered. That for me something that happened a long time ago has, in a certain weird fashion, still yet to occur? If I once thought this was an eccentricity, I am glad to now know that at the highest levels of physical science, it is shown that this may actually be the case in the way the universe unfolds/unfolded/is unfolding.

Regardless of what I thought, all I had to do was smell his body when I hugged him to be instantly drawn back all those years, as if no time had passed at all. No time at all.

Even now, I could tell you what he smelled like: leather, like the jacket he always wore, and like charcoal and cigarettes from the Larks he smoked.

Telling you of the journey is only an idle habit.
It has nothing to do with idols, nothing to do with the music.
Nothing to do with the tip of the pen on my skin.

The sun and the moon, Michael and Ethan. Ethan is fire and heat, Michael is evening and serenity. Ethan I cannot love the way he loves me, a physical attraction but without affection, and Michael could not love me the way I loved him, physical love included with the rest of what we had: the intellect, in conversations about philosophy or politics or god. With both men, I wanted lust and intellect and tenderness all. I could not separate them.

In both cases, I fell for them instantly upon meeting them, completely irrationally. With Ethan, it was pure physical chemistry: the rank smell of his body next to mine in the yoga class that first day, or when he returned home from a day of work outside under the sun, the feeling of the muscles in his legs that I caressed when I was on my knees with his penis in my mouth. With Michael it was a love born of the mind, born of talks we had about literature and music, surrounded by candles in the cold New York winter. Fuelled by the light, those talks filled me with light.

On the plane now, I am high above the planet, high over the expanse of water.

I thought I might be able to write about Michael, but every moment is filled with memories of Ethan – his voice, his body, the smell of him. The days I spent with Michael in cafés, writing or reading and talking, taking breaks to walk or to go to a museum; why have those memories come back so strongly now that I know Michael is gone? Has been gone. Is it because of what has happened or hasn't happened between Ethan and me?

The shape slowly reveals itself, I tell the story of Michael only in flashes: the day before I was leaving New York for good, Michael wrote and asked to meet. It had been months since we'd seen each other, drifting apart by coincidence, but both of us perhaps allowing the drift to carry us.

On the plane, afflicted by the night and all its attendant loneliness, I close my eyes and try to sleep. But 'night' is moving beneath me. The planet is rotating in the same direction I am flying, the planet at one thousand miles an hour and the plane at five hundred more miles an hour. We are racing into night.

What do I want? Who am I now? For the first time in my life, when I see photographs of myself, I do not recognize who I see.

So I've disappeared, not myself anymore, I am like the boy who falls into the sea at the close of Duras's *The North China Lover*; does that mean I am at last free to tell the stories in me? As for Duras, she told the story of the lover again and again: first in *The Sea Wall*, a more or less realist narrative novel, then years and years later in the impressionistic and poetic *The Lover*. After a filmmaker began adapting *The Lover* for the screen, Duras, enraged at what she saw as a romanticization of the relationship, rewrote the book as *The North China Lover*, a novel that is an account of a film that does not exist.

This year I am trying to go back to my breath, let it stretch through me. Here, hurtling through the dark under water, I want to be seen through. In *The North China Lover*, one already knows that the 'little brother,' Paulo, will die years later after Marguerite returns to France; so there, on the boat, sailing back, the nameless boy who falls overboard is somehow *also* Paulo, is also the love affair left behind, is also the reader who is about to be sent away by the writer – the book, after all, is coming to an end.

The Lover ends with the writer and lover near the end of their lives, their love still alive as ever: in other words, it ends at the end of the story. *The North China Lover* does not tell of the end of the story: instead, the boy falls into the sea. The ship to France stops for a while to search for him but eventually continues on its journey. The book ends in the middle of the journey.

My flight was early in the morning, but Ethan couldn't take me. I left for the airport before he got out of his morning shower. I wrote a little note that I was going to leave under his pillow:

When you held me in your arms I wanted to stay there for hours or days. The smell of your skin stirs my blood. Your leg against my leg. I turned to kiss your chest. I thought that outside this room I was a human being but inside this room I wanted to belong to you fully. When you came to bed you took all your clothes off and climbed into the bed in only your underwear and you wanted me to take my nightclothes off too. You did not want me to wear clothes but you did not want to make love to me. I pretended not to care just so I could be close to you longer. We slept curled in each other's arms. I tried to stay awake as long as I could just so I could feel you. In the morning, when you went into the bathroom to shower, I crawled over on my hands and knees to where you had folded your clothes neatly next to the mirror. I took your underpants and pressed the crotch against my face to smell deeply your scent. I was aroused instantly and came messily into my hand.

I did not leave the note. I could not be so vulnerable, even after the years we had been together. I crumpled the note and stuffed it into my satchel, along with the notebook in which I have been writing, long-hand, the book about Michael.

It is the book that carries me, a vessel to hold your days.

⁓

In this in-between silent time, in the air, between continents, I want to hum without words.

Why did I leave Ethan behind? At the beginning of our relationship, after all, he was so hungry for me, taking me whenever he felt like, no matter what I was doing at the time. I would be sitting and reading a book and he would come and take the book and set it aside and then pull me toward him and begin kissing me. In the beginning, out of habit, I just allowed him to do what he wanted. I liked being desired. He was so insistent, rough even, and for some reason I relented always, so easily set aflame by the flame of another. But by the end, I wasn't sure if it was me that he wanted or just another person, and I believe he didn't know whether it was him that I wanted or just another person.

I think of the photograph of me against the tree trunk, how the photographer found me beautiful but I could see only the flaws. I think Ethan should still find me beautiful, but he knows all my flaws.

—

I drew cards the night before I left. Hanging Man. I drew the Chariot after and then the Devil and then the Tower. I know what it all meant: it is time to release myself from the bondage of old and unhelpful habits. For me that is always seeking fulfillment from others. I drew all three of Ethan's cards – the Three, the Five, and the Knight of Cups – in addition to my card, the Page of Coins, and Michael's card, the Knight of Swords.

So maybe the story of Michael is not really the story of Michael but of how I responded to what Michael could not give me. The way my life now feels sometimes like the story of how I live through what Ethan cannot give me.

I rouse in the dark and switch on the seat light. I pull out the notebook from my satchel and turn to the title page. I had written there *Michael: A Novel*. I cross out *A Novel* and write *An Effacement*.

—

When one reads the story of something in a book, one thinks of the way memory changes us, the way our relationships in the past never stay what they are supposed to be but transform into sculptures like this: great elemental things, hewn from wood, not pieces of wood but entire trunks – chunks sheared off, ravines cut deeply in, titanic and alarming.

The hand or chisel of the artist is in them, you can see the grain of the blade and lathe, you can *smell* them, the living wood shaved free.

The smell of Ethan, on his skin, in his clothes, as he held me in the night.

—

As I drift again into sleep, I think about all the stories from the past, the threads that bind us. Do they bind us or can we weave with them? Does one weave with one's hands to make a text or with one's tongue? Is the structure of the story composed or does it flow in an improvisation?

Why all the fuss about 'finding your voice'? Why shouldn't we just tell our music the way we know how?

The writer himself in a relief too real to be real. The way French writers write the stories of their own lives but call them *romans*: novels. 'Autofiction,' I've heard it described as. 'Autotheory.' Or are those the same?

And the painting or the sculpture or the poem – it's just a record of the artist interacting with the surface. The materials (paint, plaster, language) irrelevant finally. In the end, is it 'writing' or 'painting'?

—

Dream: I climb a hill to find the sea. A boat rising up from the red earth to carry me away.

The beach in the rain. The rain is bright, the stones shine, but the colours are muted – of the flowers, of the people's clothes.

Dalí: 'My mysticism is not only religious but also nuclear, hallucinogenic, the mystic qualities of gothic cubism, alchemical and strange.'

There are spaces in the human torso objects can pass through. Is it possible for two people to share the same body?

Writing appears in the faces of prophets but also in the face of a mountain.

An expulsion or explosion of texture, ink, and colour: Who are we travelling up this hill, looking for the sea?

—

And what if I were to truly write the story of Michael? Maybe I'm working in the wrong medium. Maybe it shouldn't be a story in language but a black-and-white film. With a scratchy soundtrack heard through rain. How can you approximate such scale in ordinary prose?

How can life fade out even while you are looking at it? It's not the painted subjects that disappear but the world around them that disappears into them. So that you're not looking at anything anymore.

I always think I leave home in order to think. Then why am I so lonely? I can't be where I am, so I wonder and wander. But I have a home, don't I?

—

Once, after a party, Michael came back to my room with me and stayed the night. He lay on his back and let me wrap myself around him. He looked up out the window at the moonlight and talked about Baudelaire and stroked my hair. At one point I felt myself get hard against his hip and I tried to pull away, but he tightened his grip around me and pulled me closer against his body. 'Stay,' he whispered. 'This is what I can give you.' And we slept like that all night, my cheek resting on his chest, my arm thrown over his stomach, his right arm looped between my neck and shoulder, holding me against him, his left hand stroking my hair and face; he would not release me.

—

He comes and goes in my memory, across borders, into and out of lives, open and kind, a boy made from light.

The morning after he left, I lay in the bed alone, the sheets still smelling of Michael, and was crushed by endless time.

Not just the years of loving Michael and not being able to have him completely, but the years of alienation and distance and rejection from my family – all of it passed in my skin in one minute.

The interior cabin lights come back on. The flight attendants stir and come down the aisles with their carts bearing water and coffee and tea. We will soon arrive in India. Every place is home or no place is.

But the loss stemming from childhood, it won't go away.

And I shift, still in discomfort from the awkward clothes I have always worn, the terror of the self I have always despaired from.

What I thought was: Why such a long journey? Why not go home? I do have a home now, my own. I made it myself.

-3-
PRAKRITI

I arrive in Mumbai late in the Indian evening and fly on to Chennai the next morning. The festival sends a car to get me and take me to the house where I will be staying. I empty my pockets on the dresser and sleep for a few hours before the reception for the visiting writers that evening at a garden restaurant. Even though I have only just arrived, the topic of conversation turns to where I should go next, in the weeks I have between this festival and the next one. One writer insists I go to Candolim in Goa, where the beach is beautiful and a film festival will be happening; another says I should go to Hampi, several hours north of Bengaluru by car, full of monstrous boulders and carved sculpture.

Most of the evening, I avoid the other writers because I am exhausted by the bantering dinner-party repartee everyone seems very proficient with. For my part, I find myself with nothing too intelligent to say. Though there is one woman, a small stout woman named Laxmi, who I like and who has been assigned to accompany me to my readings at the various colleges. She chaperones me around the room, introducing me to this writer and that writer and constantly bringing me little plates of treats.

As the night wears on, I retreat to the kitchen, where the staff that made the dinner is eating, along with two of the foundation workers, a young man named Charles, who has moved from Durban, in South Africa, to study Indian classical drum, and who I think is probably gay, and a small birdlike woman named Aditi, in an impeccably pleated sari, who has moved here from Kochi to sing. Besides her work during the day for the foundation, she sings commercial advertisements in Tamil for radio and television. I'm more comfortable with them than with all the professors and poets lingering over their cups, declaiming and discussing.

Aditi eats with her right hand, more delicately than I could ever do, and Charles bursts out laughing whenever I say something, even if I haven't meant to be funny. At first it is off-putting, but soon I begin laughing too, and then Aditi does, and soon we are all laughing, even the kitchen staff who don't speak English.

The next morning at breakfast, the maid is annoyed with me, and her annoyance grows when I turn down a second helping of food and a second cup of chai. The woman who owns the house gestures me into the sitting room while the maid loudly clears the table, muttering under her breath, dishes clattering with her anger.

'She is upset with you. You left your money out on the dresser last night. You must not leave your money out,' the landlady says. 'She thinks she will be accused of stealing it if you lose some.'

I would never think that, I assure the landlady, but she shakes her head, waving her hand at me. 'The mistake was not hers, but yours,' she says, as if explaining something to a child. 'She does not trust you. She thinks you do not like her. Put your money away from now on.'

From then on, the maid only ever pours me half a cup of chai. When I protest, the maid replies in a facetious tone, and the landlady explains,

'She says you never want more food so she is being careful not to waste anything or give you more than you want.'

I call the car to drive me down to Mahabalipuram, where the Chola stone temples are, and to Puducherry, where the French ruled for a while. I had an old friend, Susan, from the dance company I used to perform in who moved with her husband to live at Auroville. I don't know how to reach her, but for some reason I imagine I might be able to track her down.

It is a long drive – there are no highways here, so everything is on a country road – and on the way I try my simple Hindi with the driver, but no one this far south speaks Hindi, or they don't want to, and I don't speak a lick of Tamil or Telugu, so we rely on what English he can muster.

Through the stone temples of Mahabalipuram I walk. From the shore where the receding ocean once revealed six submerged temples, thought all these thousand years to be imaginary, to the temple of Vishnu, where the boar-headed god stands in utthita hasta padangusthasana, and beside him Lakshmi, her yoni fondled and kissed by supplicants over millennia to smooth blackness.

On the tableau of Arjuna's Penance, the prince himself stands in vrksasana to receive favours, and below him in the profusion of stone animals is a cat, also standing in the posture, and around his feline feet is, the guide explains to me, a crowd of mice rejoicing that the cat has become an ascetic and thus vegetarian.

Past the tourist areas, I manage to evade my guide and discover a whole complex of additional temples carved into the enormous boulders, ruined staircases, and ancient roads winding up into the rocks, leading to startling vistas of the Bay of Bengal and the ocean.

It reminds me of a time when I was teaching in Laramie, Wyoming, and the students took me up into the mountains, and when everyone else in the large group wanted to turn back, find a tavern with warm food, I wanted to continue on the path into the night. They left me with a promise that I would walk only fifteen more minutes and then I would turn around and follow them back.

I fully intended to break the promise, I knew it, even as I was making it. I wanted to walk for an hour or more. I knew they would have to wait for me in the parking lot.

But they hadn't been gone for two minutes when the deep loneliness of stone stole into me. The aspens in the wind sounded like people talking casually, and I was sure my human spirit was too small and would vanish into the ancient pre-Columbian graffiti we had seen scrawled on the underside of one of the boulders among the fire smudges and the etched slashes.

I turned quickly back and raced to catch up with them.

In some ways, I feel like I never did catch up with them. I'm still lost there somehow, in that in-between time, the sounds of tree voices all around me.

It began because I wanted to be alone, because the sound of another breathing – *thinking* – felt like an interruption for me. But left alone among the aspens, among the boulders, with the waves, like any time I face the world alone, whether it is silence or wildness, I could not bear it.

—

We go on to Auroville, and the driver parks at the café near the big parking lot at the edge of the compound. It's a whole town really. I hadn't known that. Though there are three thousand residents and it seems impossible, I determine I will find Susan. I go into the café and ask the worker, a German woman in a cotton sari, if they know her. The worker lets me use the phone, an old-fashioned dial-up with a spiral cord, to call the main operator.

Within fifteen minutes Susan is pulling up in an auto rickshaw and we spend the afternoon driving through rice fields. She takes me to her house and we sit and look at old pictures from our dancing days. Susan looks nothing like I remember her. She's grown her hair out long and she sits on the floor like an Indian.

In the last dance we did together, we both played drunks, drunks who could not escape their drunkenness and moved sluggishly under the influence of that heaviness. The lighting was so blue, our figures were only shadows. The choreographer used Aimee Mann's song 'Wise Up.' The character I danced was able to free himself at the end of the dance, but Susan's character sank down into the pools of blue.

Now we sit in the rainforest and drink turmeric tea. She must be the blondest woman in Tamil Nadu. She sings to me what she remembers of the song and I dance what I remember of the choreography.

It feels strange, dancing those langorous movements of resignation, here across oceans and continents from the despair I once tried to give shape to. And yet that's what I try to do now, in language rather than the body. In a certain way, I miss dance. It was simpler to despair in gesture than to try to give words to feelings.

—

On the way back to Chennai, the driver stops at a roadside restaurant so we can eat. I've been instructed by my landlady that I am to give the driver some rupees for his lunch, but instead I ask him to go inside with me and sit at my table and eat. The landlady had been adamant I not do such a thing, but if the driver perceives it as out of the ordinary he does not say. Throughout the meal I ask him questions about his family and his life, but he answers only very vaguely, so eventually I stop asking.

—

When I was commissioned to read my poems at five different colleges in five days, I didn't know that 'college' meant junior high school in India. The schools I read at are all-boys schools, and the students are rowdy. The teachers quiet them down enough to listen to me, but I don't know what they hear. They are all very excited to see Laxmi, who is a frequent visitor. They call her 'Poetry Aunty.' Though Laxmi has lived in Chennai for twenty years and can speak Tamil, she neither reads nor writes it. She was born and raised in Kerala and speaks and reads and can write in Malayalam but writes poetry only in English. I cannot think of another place in the world where one could be a fluent speaker but reasonably be considered 'illiterate' in the official language of one's home state, write poetry in one's second language, and still be respected as a college lecturer.

Each day there is an evening event – a dinner, a dance performance, a reception with other writers. There is a young man named Davis who comes to nearly every event. He is small and scrawny with messy hair, and wears the same clothes – a black ribbed tank top and dirty baggy jeans – to every event. He always stands and asks a question during the question-and-answer period. His question is never interesting, it's always meandering; sometimes he hardly gets to a question. His coal-black hair is lank and greasy, and he smiles easily. Charles and Aditi are annoyed by him. Everyone else seems to tolerate him, but the moderators often cut him off while he is speaking. I find him very charming. I talk to him every evening. He loves poetry, but his knowledge seems to end with British romantic poets. He quotes Byron and Keats to me, but I wish it were Wyatt or Vaughan.

———

Most evenings there are poetry readings at bookstores at which one or two of the poets here for the festival will read. The audiences are small – devoted but small – perhaps twenty or thirty people.

One night we go to a slam performance at a local high school. Even here, in Chennai, slam performance is far more popular than traditional poetry readings: the auditorium is packed to capacity the night of the slam performance. There are hundreds and hundreds of people waiting to hear the poets. There is a slam poet from America who has come to judge and she is tall – six feet or maybe more. Her brother has accompanied her on the trip and he is taller still. After the winner, a slender high school boy, is announced, the photographers gleefully ask the tall poet and her – taller – brother to kneel up next to the winning boy. The poet on her knees is level with the boy, but the brother is, even on his knees, still taller.

There is a dinner after the reading, and one of the other visiting poets, a man named Ardeshir, long-limbed and lanky, with a head of impossibly silver curls, chooses me to receive his attention. He sits next to me and monopolizes my conversation the entire night. He has published many books and is a university professor, and it appears he feels he is favouring me, that I should know he is favouring me, that he is doing me a favour by sparing me from having to make conversation with the others, and frankly, I'm grateful for it. He keeps me laughing by making biting observations under his breath about each of our tablemates.

Every time someone tries to talk to me, he interrupts. At one point, when the ponderous filmmaker who insists I go to Goa once again begins waxing at length about the beaches at Candolim, Ardeshir somehow senses my eyes glazing over and just takes my shoulder and spins me back toward him physically, his eyes sparkling at my discomfort.

Everyone is intent on feeding me, but since my dancing days, I haven't liked food very much and sometimes have to force myself to eat it, and fried food especially makes me ill quickly. Still, I am conscious of not wanting to be rude, and so I eat a little.

Santosh, the chair of the Department of Comparative Literature at the University of Madras has had a whisky or two and is feeling ebullient. 'You must come to India! We will hire you on our faculty as a reader in translation!'

'Bengalis,' mutters Ardeshir out of the side of his mouth, nudging me in the ribs.

'They can't hold their liquor?' I ask.

'No,' he says merrily, 'they *can and do. That's* the problem!'

At the end of the night, exhausted by my unsuccessful effort to decline extra servings without seeming rude, feeling nearly sick from overeating, I excuse myself to another room to just sit and clear my head.

Ardeshir follows me in, his expression sorrowful. He knows I want to be alone but still he seeks me out. In spite of myself, I turn to him.

'I had a friend once,' he says slowly, his gaze lingering over my face. 'He was twenty-seven. We lived together. His family hated him and so I took him in. He took drugs. I tried to save him. He walked out into the street. I still don't know if it was because he was high or if he wanted to die. Maybe it was both. When the car hit him, he fell and struck his head. He did not wake up. It's been years. But since that day, nothing in the world gives me any pleasure.'

A 'friend,' I think. Who Ardeshir loved. Who probably loved him back. Michael.

The news came from Elizabeth. Michael is dead.

I sat at the dining room table, staring at the vase of lilies wilting next to my copy of The Lover.

The faucet in the kitchen was dripping.

The strange opening of that book, Duras's face: devasté. Not 'ravaged.' Maybe 'ravished' could have been a closer translation, though it too means something different – in fact, nearly opposite.

The sound of water dripping can wake me from sleep while cars in the street do not.

I look up at Ardeshir, not sure what to say, not sure if anything can be said. He looks at me a moment longer and then turns and returns to the dining room where the others are standing up, everyone preparing to leave in the waiting cars.

———

On our last night in Chennai, there is a dance performance. We sit cross-legged on tiered benches at an outdoor pavilion near the beach. Davis is there, dressed the same, leaning languidly across two levels, his elbows propping him up, his legs stretched out. Aditi scoffs, 'Look at all the space he takes!' I don't want to confess to her that I can't take my eyes off him.

Because it's Michael's body. Skinny but long. Small waist but wide shoulders, much wider than mine. Michael's body. Which isn't in the world anymore. Michael's body, which he carried out of the world.

After the performance, Aditi prepares to go back to her dormitory, which is on the beach and was one of the dorms flooded during the tsunami that revealed the submerged temples, but I convince her and Charles to go with me to a hotel bar a few blocks away. We walk down the busy street, Aditi and Charles both hefting camera equipment that they refused my offer to help with. We go into the hotel and order our drinks. Everyone stares at us. 'It's me,' says Aditi. 'Women don't normally go to bars here, and it's twice a scandal because I am wearing a sari.'

I like the picture we make, two gay men and a soberly dressed woman, drinking gin-and-tonics and being stared at.

—

Some days I imagine I could stay in Chennai. It has an easy pace and a nice warm winter. I never stay in places long enough to know if I could love them. Mornings I walk through the gardens of the Theosophical Society and evenings I stroll on the beach.

After our drink, we go to a beachfront place and eat coconut curry off banana leaves. I could live here. When I leave here, I will leave a version of myself behind that decided to stay. I have a second life, a ghost who lives here and has forgotten all about Ethan, about Michael, about writing.

—

I met Michael at a party my friend Mary was throwing that she called Une saison en enfer after the Rimbaud work, and we were all meant to dress as devils of different kinds. I went with my ex-boyfriend, who I still loved but who no longer loved me. We painted ourselves with orange body paint and spent the night talking to other people.

What I suspect: the room exists before the four walls are built. The season of hell already burned with the poem that gave shape to it and the party, in the mountains of the Hudson Valley that summoned it.

Michael was in the bathroom when I went in to put on my body paint. He was fumbling with lipstick and pencil and I took charge of him, applying the pencil thickly under his eyes, in the Persian style, and the black lipstick to his mouth. Later, after the party was over, we reconvened there and I washed his face and then I stripped off my clothes and climbed into the tub and he washed my body clean of the body paint.

What children know: there is something holy in every object or being.

As he washed me, I felt anointed. Can I go to a place I know where Michael is alive still and pouring water over me?

-4-
NORTH CLIFF

Evening in Kerala. The ocean is warm.

The plane ride from Chennai was fast and easy. Not many people fly here. The airports are quiet. There was a young man, maybe mid-twenties, sitting next to me on the plane who had never flown before. He had no suitcase, no carry-on. He held his ticket in his hand. I had to show him how to use the seat belt; he had never used one before. He kept gazing over my shoulder out the window at the workers on the tarmac loading the luggage. I asked him if he wanted to sit in the window seat and he shrank back a little.

'You should sit at the window seat,' I told him. 'You should look down at the land as we fly.' He mouth opened in a little 'o' of surprise or awe. We switched seats. 'Look down,' I whispered in his ear after we were airborne. He shrank back against me, pressing his thin torso against mine, all while leaning forward and peering out the window. He told me his name was Surya. It's an older version of the name Suraj. It means sun. His face was innocent and beautiful.

Later, as we were getting off the plane, he looked lost.

'Where do you need to go?' I asked.

He didn't answer me.

'Do you know where you are staying?'

He shook his head. 'I do not have anywhere to go.'

I gave him two thousand rupees. I wrote on the back of his ticket 'Varkala.'

—

I sink into the mood of the water, the water of the Arabian Sea. I had planned to stay in Kerala for five days only, and then travel up the coast. I'm not due in Hyderabad for several weeks yet. And there I have several more free weeks after that before I must be back in Mumbai for my flight home. At Ardeshir's insistence I booked a room at a hotel owned by friends of his, high on the bluffs of the South Cliff, set back from the main town and with a private stair down to a secluded section of the beach.

This portion of the beach is where the pilgrims from the nearby Janardhana temple come to bathe themselves. They do not remove their clothes but enter the water fully clothed, in pants and shirts, or saris, or salwar kurtas.

I feel like I am the only person alive. Certainly it feels like I am the only person staying at the hotel, the halls are so empty and dark. I go down alone for dinner, am served by nearly everyone on the staff, each trying to prove their worth as I sit distractedly on the lawn, looking down the cliff toward pitch-blackness and the roar of the water.

I was a sensitive boy. I remember crying often. Only my mother could tolerate me then and convince me that whatever had driven me to tears was small and meaningless.

It's so boring to think that all our dramas go back to childhood. If it's true, it is even sadder because there's so much we don't get to know –

unless it is the separation that we are mourning. That as a family we had been together and were suddenly splintered.

My mother is gone. I look down at the watch on my wrist. She has transformed, like those butterflies. I remind myself to take the watch off before I walk into the ocean. I wonder what it would feel like to keep walking, toward the horizon, keep walking forever.

My first glorious sunset over the western ocean and I am so exhausted from walking around all day today that I can't even raise my head to look at it. Reminds me of the time the aurora borealis could be seen in the small town in northern New York where I'd lived at the time, and everyone in our apartment was out on the small balcony looking at it, but I couldn't even rouse myself to walk ten feet.

Varkala is perched on a cliff overlooking the Arabian Sea. One has to walk down about a hundred stone steps to get to the sea.

Southern languages sound like water across rocks, or like strings being plucked or a rainstick being turned. Rain hitting the tin roof. Rain falling in puddles.

—

Hot December. Eventually, after talking to some of the hotel staff, I learn that it's the North Cliff where most of the fun is. Days I take an auto rickshaw to the North Cliff, where the main part of the town perches, and I take a yoga class, spend the afternoon on the beach. Evenings are my least favourite times because, dazed from the day's sun, I wander alone to dinner and then take another auto back to the hotel for a difficult, fitful sleep. I feel in the present moment a longing for how much I will miss this place when I leave. Is there any way for a human body, constantly shifting and changing, to actually exist in space for one moment so the mind can fix on the physical reality unfolding all around? Maybe it's the mind that's the real distraction from the sights and smells and sounds of the earth that the body wants to pay attention to.

I thought this morning about walking down to the church at the northern end of North Cliff where I haven't yet been so I can look out over unadulterated sea, which shines sparkling and weirdly white in the morning.

In the morning paper I read about a woman named Saraswati, who climbed the nineteen steps of the Ayyappan temple and made puja. It's in the news because it's illegal: Ayyappan, born of two gods, Shiva and Vishnu, is sacred to a men's movement here in India, and women are not allowed in his temple.

A friend invites me to Bengaluru. Should I go there or stick with my plan?

Why is it we always only want to be where we aren't? The sea is pearly white with sunlight, sparkling like little diamonds on the surface of marble or granite. I can't bear the – what? – empty days or the end of the empty days? When what I want is to go down to the beach or go back to my room and lie down in the darkness and be still.

I feel emptied out, not myself anymore. Which is why I came. If I go to Bengaluru, I will meet other people and they will remind me who I am.

⁓

Michael,

It may be a failure of empathy to even ask, but I do want to know what the last minutes are like for one whose determinations of suicide move past ideation or metaphor the way, anorexic and famished, yet determined to survive, I nonetheless paused for a whole afternoon just to wonder what it would feel like to eat before taking a bite.

These days I drift wide and alone on the rushing current of old sorrows.

The wind is so unloving and the beach lands are so far, I wish my body would refuse to float.

Michael, I wondered the whole time we were together, even though we weren't, How will Michael change me? Ought I be afraid?

How can I find out what I need to know?

That note I wrote to Ethan but did not leave for him. Unsent letters are sometimes the best kind.

—

Ayyappan was born of two men. A demon was ravaging the heavens and it was foretold that only a child of Shiva and Vishnu could defeat him. Vishnu transformed himself into the form of Mohini the Enchantress and seduced Shiva to give birth to Ayyappan. Child of two men or, depending on your view, child of a cisman and a transwoman. There is an irony in his cult refusing women the right to worship at his altar.

The woman Saraswati, herself named for a goddess and identified in the papers only by her first name, was arrested for her transgression, though eventually released with only a warning.

—

More people arrive at the hotel. I am not the only one here anymore.

The power has gone out and we are in the dark except for candles here and there. People imitate the cries of the animals and the waiters continue their service. In the distance, halfway down the hill to the little trail that leads through the rice paddies to the beach, I can hear the hotel's generator groaning to life.

For a moment we were steeped in something – suspended, out of time – and something, I don't know, drew us back to our normal life, murmured conversation, the youngest child at the table next to mine screaming because he wants the ball the others are playing with.

I miss home – not the specifics of it, but the fact of it. The hotel staff say the power will be back soon and dinner will be served. I watch the children in the swimming pool.

The children are going into the pool with their clothes on. Near as I can tell, no one has started eating yet. I will go upstairs and lie down and hope to be able to speak.

If only there were English breakfast – porridge, beans, and toast – I would be happy, but this isn't the hotel that European people come to. This is the hotel for the well-off pilgrims with families, who don't need to stay in the guest houses lining the stone staircase from the temple into the town on the cliff. The rich Europeans stay down at the place near the rice paddies, in little faux huts with in-house masseurs. The younger tourists and backpackers stay up on the cliff.

I miss the life of the town on the cliff. There are no street lights, so I cannot walk along the beach to get there. I will leave the curtains open and wake with the sun.

One could sit in the lobby here with some coffee and be perfectly anonymous.

All the lights come back on. The children are quiet. Everyone eats. Comforting sound of gentle clicking and clattering of silverware and dishes.

I feel like a character in a Duras novel, abstract personality, giant empty hotel overlooking the sea, days unrolling their length in the heat. And so on. There is some dangerous feeling of possibility inherent in the generic.

How could it be only weeks ago that I was skidding across the leaves at the base of my driveway? Weeks ago I was with Ethan.

Time is a lovely friend. I've no heart for another beginning. Instead I am happy to be in the middle of things. My season changes too.

—

For the third time in a row, I see the same couple, an Arab woman I met one day in the yoga class and her boyfriend, newly arrived from England. Whenever I see them they are fighting. She has brought him here and I don't think he likes it, but he is trying very gamely. They are marching along on some kind of shopping mission.

She is tall, willowy, wearing a crop top that bares her midriff and low-riding billowy salwar pants, striding ahead. He is short, a cub, built like a fire hydrant, looking very out of place in T-shirt and blue jeans, practically jogging to keep up with her. The funny part is that I only ever see them marching from north to south. They must at some point walk in the other direction, but I never notice.

—

The wind comes so strong through the barred window; by the sea, storms are bearable and even secretly wished for.

Soon my claims will write themselves in another language. Soon my book of water, about Michael, in bits and pieces. Even now I feel him disappearing in the sensuality and stimulation of India.

—

Some stories I cannot yet write.

I loved Michael and I lost him.

Sometimes I wish I had been born in a different body.

—

For the first time, I stay down at the beach for the closing of it at sunset. First the sky streaks violently pink. Then the air cools and the wind picks up. The lifeguards blow their whistles and herd everyone out of the water. The beach clears out except for the Indian families who still lounge in the sand or stand just at the wrack line, all still fully dressed. They cavort, play games; the men wrestle in the sand or play volleyball or turn gymnastic flips.

The beaches are separated during the day. The tourist police don't like the local men to go into the Western part of the beach and hit on the women. Or is it that the priests from the temple do not want the Indians mixing with the naked Westerners? I'm not really clear on who has ordered the beach segregated and why. And which side of the beach do I belong on anyhow? I am lounging among the tanning Westerners, half-naked myself, when one guard, in short blue shorts and shirt sleeves, barefoot, smacking a short billy club into his palm, tries to make me put on a shirt and pants and go to the Indian side of the beach. He will not let me stay sunbathing until I show him my U.S. passport. Even my Canadian accent does not assuage him. And why am I accepting the privilege to be half-naked that my nationality offers me?

Then the light becomes a more and more intense pink, rose grey, brilliantly glowing dark like weather before or after a storm that hovers, does not disappear but lingers, lingers until nearly forgotten, and in the meantime, the ocean roaring all the time, it's become dark.

The lights blink on, the music comes on, the cafés and restaurants above on the cliff start to fill. The thundering surf continues, insisting on itself, but we mostly don't hear it over the blaring of various kinds of music in every language from around the world.

The immense dark of the ocean is sequined, its billowing endlessness fastened back by a multitude of little lights in the distance – not cities, though they could be, but fishing boats, trawling through the night, bringing in fresh kill in the morning. And farther out still, the big oil tankers.

—

I remember Anaïs Nin in Bali at the end of *Diary, Volume Four:* 'I remembered that the definition of tropic was "turning," "changing," and I felt a new woman would be born here.'

Rather than shuck everything off – this book I am failing at, my family that cannot see me, Ethan, the memories of a man who never really loved me – I pass that moment and continue on. I leave off the frenzy that has always destroyed my intentions.

Ardeshir, back at his home in Mumbai, writes to say he wants to come and teach at my college. Poor man. The death of his lover, his hypersociality masquerading as charm – after the dinner party I didn't want to see him anymore, but he phoned three times the next morning, I'm sure to reassure himself that he hadn't ruined our friendship.

He hadn't, he couldn't, because I always keep people at a distance. I keep so many people I imagine myself close with firmly at a distance.

Something about him reminds me uncomfortably of myself: the hunger, the sadness, the acting out and needing affection, so needy it expresses itself as control. And yet, in spite of this, I feel friendship and kindness from Ardeshir, who seems to be deeply interested in me and my work and to have genuine affection for me.

I struggle through the small bits of writing about Michael. It was a relationship built of ordinary days. To make a story from it, I find myself leaving most of it out. Is this what fiction is? Nothing of the ordinary in it? Though that is what our lives are made of. Even the grand plots of love and death do not really begin and end.

Reading novels about relationships is like only watching a dance, never being allowed to dance oneself.

I remember when Ethan and I were in Barcelona in 2007, we went to a performance of *Antigone* in Catalan. We were able to more fully imagine the play, hear it in a space beyond language. At the height of the Greek play, Antigone screams out in agony. It is normally transcribed as 'OIOIOIOIO' or some such onomatopoeic representation of wordless grief. But that night in Barcelona, when Antigone screamed, the actress screamed in English: 'Oh to never know the marriage bed, to never bear children – '

That moment of translation was shocking because in the original her grief has no expression but is nonsensical and immense. Which the English might have been to the mostly Catalan-speaking audience. But not to Ethan and me. We knew what had broken Antigone's heart, even if no one else did.

⁓

The sun floods in through the window in the morning, which is full of nothing but the blue of sky and water. Though faced with the sun and light of the beach, I could not rouse myself.

Yesterday I bought a tapestry from the Uttar Pradesh craft shop and didn't have money to pay for it. It is a long, thin tapestry, like a floor-length mirror, made of dramatic blues and silver-threaded throughout, beaded with little pearl-like beads. The merchant refused to wait for me to pay, wrapping up the tapestry for me to take with me anyhow. I promised to go back today and pay. It is grey today and pleasant. The sun has given us some winter relief. I decide to stay ten more days before going up to Hyderabad for the literary festival.

The fan blows through the room. The other guests who mysteriously appeared for dinner last night have drifted back into space. Anonymous places, suspension of time. A little boy playing in the pool with his father. My father leaves another message: he is going to Pakistan, he will not be back in the States when I return. As if we had planned to see each other. For some reason, in our messages we imagine that our relationship is ordinary, that nothing is wrong.

You think you know yourself so well.

Hazy out, a little sultry but a hint of a cooling breeze blowing down from the hills. The coffee's weak this morning. India knows tea, not coffee. Instead of breakfast, I go down and have an Ayurvedic massage and a sweat in the steam room.

While reading my poems out loud to the students in Chennai, I became aware of how mannered fragmentation has become for me. That it does not hurt to ground a lyric poem – just a small bit – with pronouns or actual narrative situation.

My new book is meant to be a celestial book of spirit-in-matter. Going back to where I started but fully new.

It shouldn't be *Michael: An Effacement*. I'm not 'effacing' him; I'm trying to see something about my life *through* his death.

I cross out the word *Effacement*. But what do I replace it with?

I have discovered that I don't need to take an auto to the North Cliff. If I walk up the stone ramp to the plaza where the temple is, I can cross over to that strand of cheap hotels, yoga studios, cafés, and tourist shops. There are restaurants and bars open late at night and steps – I counted them, one hundred and eight – to the sea.

The sea, which stretches incredibly forever. I cannot explain why every sea has this effect on me. I sit at one of the cafés, facing it. I ask for more coffee. Since there are so many tourists here from different places, the menu has separate sections: Indian, English, French, Israeli, Swedish, and Russian. I choose from the Israeli menu: shakshuka.

The young man with whom I journeyed on the plane from Chennai to Trivandrum has just drifted by on the walkway. He saunters along, smiling, still wearing the same clothes he wore on the plane. 'Surya!' I call after him. He does not hear me. He disappears down the road.

Surya. The sun. A man who had never been on a plane before. Who is he and what is he doing on this cliff? I could ask the same questions of myself. We are not what we seem, any of us. Who am I here, a lonely son who has not yet called his father. And my father: he only wants the son he knows. Surya was smiling a smile of bliss. What had he seen? Where had he been? What is he doing here without any clothes but the ones on his back, maybe no money but the rupees I gave him, most of which he must have used to get here?

I never imagined I would be this lonely, though I understand how everything in my life has brought me to this.

The ocean has an answer, but it thinks I won't like it.

Let the sun enter the doors and seek you out.

What I am doing here? Am I really here to write this book or read from books already written?

One is for the future and one is for the past, though which might be which keeps changing in my mind.

Can writing ever really be in the present tense?

This morning. The ceiling fan turning. The enormous banana tree next to the building, a pendulous flower hanging just next to the window.

It was Surya in the present tense earlier this morning, walking down the road, that smile on his face, nothing in his hands, his mind on the moment, not wondering, 'How will I explain this later?'

Suddenly I don't want all the extra things I've brought with me, all the clothes, all the books. I pack up everything I can, everything I think I really don't need, into a box to ship back to the States. The hotelier sends me with one of the workers on a scooter into town, where I have the box sewn up in canvas, sealed by glue gun, then addressed in fat markered letters. We scoot off to the post office, me balancing the box on my knees, the boy weaving his scooter in and out of traffic. He smiles constantly but doesn't speak any English or Hindi, and I don't speak any Malayalam, so our friendship is entirely through facial expression and touch. His name is Suraj. Sun.

Someday, when no one is looking, Surya and Suraj are going to meet. See, that's what you can do in fiction. I could write a novel in which the two men meet, one completely unaware, informed by ancient traditions and shining like a lamp in a modern world, and the other exhausted and cynical but knowledgable and world-wise. I would want them to meet. I want them to love each other.

Was that Michael and me? *Michael, you are a boy falling from the sky. Sing all the way down.*

Surya and Suraj. Well, that's as far as I've got. There's no actual plot. There aren't even any words yet. So what: I can't think of any words.

Another yoga class. Christine, the Arab woman, tells me if I'm staying in Kerala longer that I should take a boat into the backwaters, that she and her boyfriend, Mark, went for an overnight journey and it was magical waking up on the water. I think that if Ethan were here, he would go with me.

I belong to no one here and no one belongs to me.

So what about this place, so beautiful, so full of water and light. How can it exist and I not share it with Ethan?

The afternoon sun on the diamonded sea. I dream always of water.

Boys fall from the sky here and drown because they disobey their fathers.

And other sons kill their fathers. Must the journey of the son be always this: Kill or die?

Then there is Saraswati, the woman who dared to climb the steps of the temple of Ayyappan to make her puja. Why would she, knowing the consequences?

If only I had a shot at explaining.

The newspapers did not give her last name.

So we go on the way we do, silenced, enraged at the refusal of the other to reconcile.

The small of your back. My hand on your back pulling you close.

A man sits by the stone ramp selling maps. Though what map could tell me where to go?

Someone in Chennai, when they were introducing me, called me 'a poet of experience.' I wanted to say: 'The Hudson was my professor. Taught me about body, beauty, locality, and god.'

Kerala, place of water. I am made of fire and air, that's why I wanted to stop here, stop moving, flow in and out.

But I can't stay more, I think the sound of the water has already expressed it, or maybe not its sound but its vocabulary.

How did I become a poet anyhow but by insisting on the uniqueness of the word and the real power of its music unleashed in mosaic context?

Long lines of the flaming surf, pink sunsets roll in over the grey.

I walk north along the cliff in silence.

Winter solstice is tomorrow. I'm not due in Hyderabad until after the new year.

I cancel everything: my Kochi arrangements, my hotel in Mangalore, I email the professors from Chennai and say I am not going to Candolim. I stop in at one of the guest houses that line the cliff and book another fortnight.

I am staying in Varkala.

—

Having decided to stay, I wonder how it is I know I belong in a place or to a place.

At any rate, these are small things to sing about. Why should I always be looking to some idea of god? Is it that I am trying to prove something to my father?

When the fan is running, the night is pleasant and I feel sweet loneliness to be so far from home.

I leave another message for my father, telling him that I am in India. Somehow I imagine it would please him, though it is my mother who really cared about being from India. And she's gone. And all the nostalgia in my poetry, all my grubbing after god, what if it is only a way of telling my father I am worth something?

We don't believe the same things, and so much time has passed. It is already too late for what I am trying to do. We have already lost all we could have had.

—

Michael said if he could have a superpower he wanted those of the dragon: to fly, to breathe fire.

For me, I would like to be able to change into what surrounds me. When in water, I would like to be able to become water. When buried alive, I would like to be able to become stone. I want to be able go down inside the chasm. And live.

—

I'm part failure now.

When we went to Pakistan in 1983, we stayed with my father's younger brother and his family: his wife and three sons. The five of them and my mother and I all lived in their two-room apartment. Some days I went to visit two second cousins whose father was wealthy. They lived in a walled mansion in the Defence district. Our second cousins had their own apartment within the mansion, each with their own bedroom, plus a sitting room, and their own bathroom, air conditioning, and plush furniture. We would spend all day reading Archie comics and talking and laughing. Breakfast and lunch were brought up to us, but we always had to dress and go down for dinner. Though the big house below was air-conditioned, the stairwell was not, and we always hurried through the sultry air as fast as we could.

One night my father flew to Pakistan to surprise us. We hadn't seen him for almost three months, and I can't ever remember being happier than waking up and seeing his face.

The next day, my boy cousins were all off from school. I was really unhappy to be stuck in the tiny sweltering apartment with ten other people while I knew my cousins were enjoying the cool comforts of iced sodas and stacks of Archie comics.

At this point I realized that *my* family wasn't 'rich,' even in the States. And I wished we were. I wished we had more. I told all this to my father. He tried to explain to me that we always had enough, that my cousins were so happy to just have me there for the day with them. To this day I still feel ashamed that I wanted to go visit our rich cousins instead, that I had ever in my life even for a minute made my father feel badly for not providing for us, for disappointing him.

Oh, just you wait, I think back to my child self. *There's a lot more of that on the way.*

―

One thinks in the rhythms of the ocean in the little cliffside town. Suddenly I think, here in the sun and water, why should I write a book about the death of love, why should I write about Michael, someone I knew so long ago and then didn't know at all?

When I could write another novel, a different one of this very moment – that this joy could at last answer, it could reclaim the space from death and abandonment. How would I write a book like that? How would I begin?

Oh, but again: *words*. Better to do what I am doing: live in the body, translate, write, be awake without processing and distilling.

The ocean never leaves you. The sun never leaves you.

My first book was not poetry at all but a novel, written in little fragments. A man at the seaside who does not know whether or not he will return to his life. A man who much resembles me, and who drowns at the end of the book – or maybe doesn't?

He walks into the water at the end of the book but does not again emerge. The last sentence of the book is the single word 'Breathe.' As far as I know, only one person in the world has ever read the little book. Some months after it was published – with not one review, not one single person showed up at the reading I gave for its release – I received a letter from an old woman who lived in a house in Provincetown at the end of Cape Cod, which is where the book is set. She wrote that I had 'captured' the essence of Provincetown, in her words 'its light and wind.' I liked the idea that the most important thing about a book was not its character nor its plot but its *mood*.

Then she went on to say that she had only one single suggestion – that she thought the last line ought to have read 'Breathe?'

It was a suggestion that startled the breath out of my body. It threw the ending wildly open. It changed the tone of the entire book.

Though there was never a second printing – the book quietly sank to the bottom of the ocean – I always thought I would make that revision, that it was truer than the ending I had originally written.

Though in my mind, he disappeared into the depths here in Varkala, I could imagine writing a sequel in which the man resurfaces, having chosen to live. He would resurface not in the ocean where he went under but somewhere else, far from here, perhaps in the north; he would emerge instead from the solid earth, clawing his way out, chthonic, on the road between Delhi and Dehra Dun.

He wouldn't even be the main character of the sequel. The new character would be sitting somewhere, perhaps at a café, maybe a café high up like this one, but inland: on a rooftop, overlooking a forest. And the sun would glint and the drowned man would rise up out of the ground, fully clothed, described exactly as he was at the end of the other book, seventeen years ago, not having aged a day.

He would climb the steps up to the terrace and walk past the characters of the new book, trailing dirt and earth, saying nothing to them, passing by on his way into whatever comes next.

Was I *always* writing about Michael, even when I thought I wasn't?

—

The sea such a light blue and grey, like a mourning dove. My intention this morning was to find a place to sit and write more in the book. So what if there was no epic love story? So what if there was no dramatic action, no sinking into the ocean nor rising up out of it? My life with Michael was ordinary, the most special moments were *ordinary*, so let me write the ordinary.

—

Scrub the dishes, sweep the floor. Michael is asleep and I am in his kitchen, cleaning.

I watch people walking by, their boots and shoes passing on the sidewalk.

I hear him breathing. I lie down next to him. He moves against me. His arm around me. He kisses my ear.

He lets me lie next to him, be against his body. It is enough for me.

The tiles of the backsplash have been washed. Michael doesn't like to use chemical cleaners, so I clean his dishes and backsplash with warm water and vinegar.

I'm done for.

I'd rather be here cleaning than at home, waiting for his call.

Who lives in this mess?

Who is the boy whose body encircles mine?

When I am at home, I wait for Michael's knock on the door. When I am with Michael, I am waiting for him to wake up.

⁓

Rain-smeared pages, long and drawn-out breakfast, no lunch but water and juice.

Christine and Mark were having another epic battle in the stairway before yoga class, I don't know about what; I always try as hard as I can to filter out the actual words, only register the sound of their voices, rising in tension. I walked down with them after the class ended and they seemed fine while we were chatting, but later I saw them fighting in the street.

⁓

But it is hard to be the other person arriving. Once, when Ethan visited me in Pennsylvania, I made a disaster of the weekend by accepting an invitation to dinner with people he didn't know. He's uncomfortable around strangers, he doesn't like it when plans change, and he was sad because he wanted to spend the time with me alone. Well, it is a sunny day, the last of the year, somewhere on the other side of the world Ethan is ringing a bell. I hope he hears me singing back.

⁓

New Year's Eve. I go to the one nightclub they have here and it is terrible. From across the room I see Surya, the boy from the plane. He is dancing with glee. He has taken off his collared shirt and is wearing just his white undershirt, which clings to his chest and torso. I try to make my way toward him, but he disappears in the crowd.

Before I can search for him longer, Christine shows up with the boyfriend in tow, hurrying to keep up with her long-legged stride. They are going to climb down the stairs in the dark. 'You should come with us,' Mark says. Without thinking, I agree, and we are halfway down the stairs when I realize it is perhaps a bad idea and that, like Ethan in Pennsylvania, Christine maybe does not want me to come, that they should go down to the beach as a couple.

But it is too close to midnight, and I don't want to go back up in the dark, and Christine is talking about the moonlight, so I continue with them. We find a place to sit and look out at the roaring ocean. Mark has brought a bottle of champagne and some plastic cups. He pops the cork and pours us each a little.

We sit there before the ocean and watch the new year come in. We are happy, they are happy with me there, maybe that is why Mark invited me, why Christine did not object: they need someone else between them to be happy.

⁓

Hot January morning, I rise early before sunrise, walk along the beach still cluttered with the litter of last night's revelry. The sky turns the sharpest pink.

What I should be doing now is sleeping on the beach, but instead I am drinking coffee, reading a beat-up novel I found in the used bookstore tucked behind a tailor's shop. The book is called *Indian Nocturne* by Antonio Tabucchi. The narrator is doing what I'm doing, travelling across India, though he is in search of a friend who has gone missing, while I am trying to escape, but from what – from the ghost of Michael? The remnants of my relationship to my family? Or from the impending ruin of my relationship with Ethan?

Tabucchi can write the story because he is Italian and so for him India is a strange place. The novel has no plot. It meanders as the narrator meanders. Or perhaps it's more accurate to say that the plot *is* the journey. The missing friend seems like just an excuse for him to wander. But who am I in India, land of my forebears? Which nonetheless does not want me, a Muslim, still after these long centuries an 'invader'?

There *is* a reason I came to India to write about Michael. Because I needed distance from Ethan, because I needed to be someplace new, but someplace where I would still be surrounded by the language I live in. And yet I fail. All I can write about Michael are episodes, flashes. There's nothing holding it together. But in our life together there was nothing holding *us* together. And in the end, there was nothing holding Michael together either.

The ocean has had enough of my fickle ways and sends its demands to me in rays, the sun in waves. We have all begun speaking one another's language.

I leave the novel on the table in the café and go back to the tailor's shop and get measured for shirts, Indian-style kurtas, one waist-length, one falling to the mid-thigh, and another longer to the knee. I choose the colours of spring: pink, yellow, and light green.

By the time I return, the book is gone, taken by another diner or thrown away as trash, I do not know. And do not mind, really. I do not wish to know whether the narrator finds his friend or not. If he does find him, I don't see how it would avoid being anticlimactic. If he *doesn't* find him, that too would come as a disappointment, probably more than I could bear.

—

I saw the sun over the darker and darker sea. Then it became only sound. And because you cannot see it, it is louder.

The town is more cluttered suddenly. In the dark. The mint lemonade tastes like it has been cut with tap water.

After yoga class today, Christine was on her way to the Ayurvedic hospital, so I go along. While she goes in for her treatment and Mark goes upstairs for Thai yoga massage, I sit down with Kamaraj, the resident physician.

'What is your ailment?' he asks, as if I have one.

I think. What *is* my ailment? 'I have a friend who died,' I say, as if that counts.

He waits.

'And my father does not know how to love me.'

He does not say anything. He waits.

Do these count as 'ailments'?

I continue. 'He loves me but he does not love all of me.'

The ocean still roars outside.

'I can't sleep,' I say then.

He nods, writing on the notebook in front of him.

'I'm sad most of the time. Probably I drink too much.'

He continues writing.

I say, 'I don't eat.'

He looks up, sharply.

'Much,' I stammer. 'I don't really eat *much*.'

He closes the book and stands. 'Come,' he says.

I follow him into a smaller room that looks much like any doctor's examination room might, though it is flooded with light and ocean air blowing in through the open windows. It is dominated by a long wooden massage table, gleaming with oil. He gestures. I lie down on the table. My head and neck balance in a ridge and depression fashioned in the table, as if there were a pillow.

He pulls over a dolly from which is suspended a kind of bell or gourd with a thick wick protruding from it, and prepares me to receive the treatment called shirodhara – a constant stream of scented oil pouring down the wick and onto my third eye, the stream passing side to side.

As the oil pours, I feel as if my third eye opens and visions pour through, the stream of memories, river of my life.

A dark woman in a white sari. The train tracks running fifty feet above the street.

Ethan smiling shyly at me as we put our shoes on at the yoga studio.

Tipping Michael's face back and painting his lips black.

Now I homeward spill.

It came to me once by the river's edge.

The questions of my father are meant to be answered by my mother. And my mother is gone. So who will speak for me?

When I was a child, my father used to write little sermons for me to give at the majalis.

I was his voice and loved so being.

In Cairo he wanted to give every beggar money. He made me carry small bills. Now, in India, across an ocean, when I give money to people

– every single one who asks me, shocking my Indian friends, who disapprove – I think to myself, *It is my father who gives you this.*

I've lost him. There is no returning, but I have to try, don't I?

Who do I mean by 'him'? My father? Or is it Michael? Or Ethan?

All the love I have lost.

The trickle of thoughts is constant.

In a way the shirodhara feels the same as writing because it asks you to channel the constant wash into a trickle along a thread. One must stay along the thread to organize the oil into syntax and sentences.

My mother is saying something, but I cannot make out the words.

Language and memories stream along the wick, onto my forehead, and roll away.

—

I continue to return to the Ayurvedic hospital each day after the morning yoga class.

Some days I receive a massage with oil and sand. Other days they pound my skin with herb poultices. Other times I am given a medicinal oil in my nostrils that stings and burns. And other days, there is more shirodhara.

I've stopped wearing my glasses. Is it possible the oil massage, especially on my face, is helping to correct my vision?

Morning sun.

After a week of vigorous yoga every morning and oil massage every afternoon, my skin stinging from the herb treatments, my hunger awakens. Maybe I will eat lunch today.

The notebook in which I have been keeping the texts about Michael has sat unopened for too long. I turn to a new page and write:

I could be unfolded so easily.

Michael leaning into me, his arm around me.

I slide out from under his arm and climb over onto the other side of him.

I pull him against me. He nestles in closer. I bury my face in his wild hair.

He mumbles, 'Kiss me.'

He means the back of his neck. I kiss him.

—

The sea glimmers.

I have come from yoga class. Now I am sitting in in a little place called the Kerala Café, which overlooks the bright sea. I'm confused now about which day it is – Tuesday or Wednesday? Which means is my ticket for Friday or Saturday?

I've lost time.

I've hardly looked at the stars in the sky.

I've hardly looked anywhere but at myself. Fine, I retreated. I was looking for a life that was mine.

I am what I imagined: a man with no work but his own journey. A resonance.

There is a note from a friend, Ruman, who is studying gay nightlife in India. He is in Bengaluru for ten days and he suggests I come and meet him there before going on to Hyderabad. Sitting here, in this café on the cliff, I don't know anymore what it would feel like to re-enter the world of a city, check into a hotel, hear cars and motorcycles passing by.

The sun is red and grey, and I have to admonish myself not to stare into it.

Will I keep this feeling of peacefulness, of understanding the languages of water, when I return to all my obligations, all my promises and work?

I have a feeling, a real one, that I could choose my own life, that I really, really could. I could choose my life and it wouldn't skitter away like a frightened animal but would stay. Would wait for me.

—

Now in the lit night, a moth to my childhood flame, I wonder what I am or where I belong. A weird moment between dark and dawn when your body trembles between incarcerations.

There is a shadow on the page. I look up. Staring down at me again is that beautiful face of the innocent man from the plane. The sun has cast its shadow.

'Surya,' I say. And he sits, as if we are old friends, as if I invited him. He folds his hands on the table and looks at me. He expects me to say something. He is older than I had thought he was when we were sitting next to each other on the plane. This is the first time I am looking right at him, studying his face. He has the slender build of a much younger man.

I don't know what to say.

'I like the trees here,' I say. He smiles then, a wide smile so I can see his orange-stained mouth, his teeth and tongue tinted from chewing supari. 'Because they don't lose their leaves. Everything is green all year.'

'I like winter in India,' Surya says. 'It's not hot.'

I smile, wanting to disagree with him. After all, it's more than ninety degrees at the moment, but maybe for Surya that is indeed 'not hot.'

'I am jealous of your trees,' Surya says then. 'The trees in Amrika. They live and die and then live again. They see God from both sides.'

I don't answer. At the moment I feel like my own life has been blown open, splintered into little pieces on the ground. *Like a tree*, I think then, and for the first time, really, wonder if – like the trees, like Nin in the tropics – I too will be born once more.

Surya across from me, I think for some reason of my last trip to India, in 2010, the train's savage echo in my ear hours later in the hotel room at Tulsi Ghat in Varanasi while the Saraswati Puja raved down to the river. Hundreds of young men stripped to the waist, dancing, bearing effigies of the goddess.

A body is not a body at all but a meeting place, a prayer room where everyone sings.

'Why have you come?' I ask Surya. 'On the plane? To Kerala? When you didn't know where to come?'

He frowns, and I think perhaps he has not understood my question.

'My family sent me,' he says slowly, seeming to hesitate, as if deciding on what happened, or maybe deciding on what details he is willing to share. 'To go to Shiva Mela. They wanted to save me because I loved another boy.'

Boy, I think to myself, *means anyone who isn't married.*

'I loved my friend Louis. But Louis became married. But we still love each other. So Louis's wife's family did not want me to be seeing Louis anymore. And my uncle thought they might kill me. My heart breaks, so my uncle gave some money so I could come to Lord Shiva. My father says don't come back. My mother says come back. So I don't know.'

'His name is Louis?' I asked.

'They are French Indians,' Surya says. 'From Puducherry. Christians. I didn't go to the Shiva temple because I did not think Lord Shiva would help me. You wrote on my ticket this town name, and I came and now I want to stay here on the cliff, I want to look at the ocean because it reminds me of the water in Puducherry when Louis and I used to walk. Except here the sun comes up over the water in the morning and there the sun goes down into the water in the evening.'

'Where are you staying?' I ask.

'At the Baby Hotel,' says Surya, gesturing farther north on the cliff. 'I am going to stay and work. They are letting me stay. I clean the rooms.'

—

We walk, Surya and I, north along the cliff, past the path to the Baby Hotel, so named for its exterior painted pastel pink, past other hotels, shops, staircases down to the beach, eventually coming out at the north end of the cliff road, which slopes down to the beach. There, down a little path, stands a church. I want to go inside and look, but Surya shakes his head.

'Louis says you should not go inside a church unless you are going to worship there.'

Instead, we sit on the rocks together and watch the water.

He leans close, he tries to be charming. I am fixated by his green-flecked eyes and dark skin. At the gate to the church stands a juniper tree with little yellow blossoms. In the heat I see the ocean striking the large boulders and have a vision of Surya on the plane, fumbling the seat belt buckle, not know what it is or how it works, not knowing if he will ever see Louis again.

When you are on the ground, how do you know where you are? When I was flying from New York, the seatback screen map in front of me on my way to India had a little icon of the plane travelling over

Afghanistan into Pakistan. After some time of rushing through light, we entered the shadow of the sun. Full moon in the window of the airplane. We had caught up to the night.

We are flying over Karachi, I thought to myself at one point. My father as a child in the early 1940s is down there somewhere still, an echo of him anyhow, an incarnation.

The town slowly disappears, its edges evaporating in sheets of darkness coming over the ocean. The horizon practically glows in the weird storm light and the juniper is only a dark mark against the low wall.

I turn in no direction but loss, the sun magnet pulling me across the water to the end of the earth.

Here is how a man lives who once was a boy who dreamed of wings: always searching for the solution of what besides his father's craft might yet turn his body into another body, not yet realizing it is the language in his mouth that could yet bear him aloft, drench him in salt and sun.

I turn to Surya. I smile at him in the last light, bright and orange on our faces. He leans forward, stopping just a fraction of an inch from my face. He is looking into my eyes. I look back. I do not move. I do not cease smiling. I want there to be a kiss now but I do not want to kiss him. I want him to choose.

Then he kisses me. He is trembling with grief for his love, Louis, and he kisses me in the sun and I kiss him back because it is all that I can give to him. In this moment he either wants me to be Louis or he wants me to not be Louis, and whichever it is he wants me to be, I am willing to be that for him.

—

So I sit now at the airport, Varkala in the rear-view mirror, Surya left behind on the cliff, my body still singing with all I learned of Ayurveda and yoga from Kamaraj's treatments and yoga classes, still singing from being shone upon by Surya, his eyes always searching, his mouth twitching with unasked questions.

The last night in Varkala, Surya and I walked back along the cliff and found a restaurant near the Baby Hotel. We sat and talked together, instantly familiar. After his disclosure to me, I felt it was easy to say important things to him, about my work, my family, my life, my loneliness and sadness. His eyes stayed on me as I spoke. He did not respond or even nod or shake his head. He only listened. I told him about my father. I told him about Michael.

In this way, I always find a friend.

—

Sitting at the airport, waiting for them to announce boarding for the plane to Bengaluru, I feel dizzy, nearly sick. When I leave a place, I feel that I am leaving behind the future unfolding without me and that soon I will catch up to it and know it. But that it is happening now, in the present moment.

I am trying to have a moment of still time, but a young Indian man with shoulder-length hair, loose, sits across from me. He is beautiful in that stupid, unimaginable way that all young Indian men seem to be. He keeps looking up at me surreptitiously, then returns to his phone, typing furiously, scrolling.

I get into the ticket line. He stands behind me. I feel his attention. Finally I turn around, not kindly, and look right at him. And wait for him to speak.

'Is this you?' he asks, tentatively, holding his phone screen out toward me so I can see the multiple small thumbnails his search engine has produced of my face. 'Are you this man, the one who writes all the books?'

So. One *can* be found. The one 'who writes all the books.' Is that who I am? Rishi, as I learn, has a girlfriend who is doing a doctorate in literature, which is how he recognized me. From that moment, he takes it as a charge to take care of me, he accompanies me onto the plane, has my seat changed so I will sit next to him on the short flight. The attention is a little unsettling, but I linger in the first moment of his question: 'Is this you?' *Is* it? When I have doubts I remember that moment: staring into Rishi's eyes, without subterfuge, shocked by remembrance, alarmed at being recognized, about to board the plane, about to leave the most beautiful place I think I have ever been.

-5-
CHURCH STREET

Rishi's driver takes me to my hotel on Church Street. I chose it because I would be able to walk to the park from there and get around easily in auto rickshaws. After Rishi arranges my room, we part ways. He promises to send his car for me later in the week to bring me to his house for dinner. I thank him and start thinking of how I might get out of the commitment. Somehow being known for even a short time has made me nervous, made me miss the anonymity I had in Varkala.

Church Street is mostly a walking street, lined with hotels and restaurants and bookstores and bars, running along the arterial road that leads from here to Cubbon Park and beyond into the city.

I walk along the sidewalk, thick concrete planks balanced over the sewer.

The bellboy at the hotel, shy but always smiling, manages to take all my bags at once up the stairs. I am not permitted to help. I must be overtipping because whenever I emerge from my room, there are three or four bellboys hanging about, competing with one another to be the one I call on to help me. They get jealous and swear at each other in Kannada, and so I try to choose a different one each time.

What is this empty city but a place to find language. Empty because I am alone here, because I do not understand Kannada and know only two people, one of whom I just met and the other I have not yet met in person.

In New York once, I wrote my life down on index cards rather than in a book. It was May 2001, late spring, and I was finishing school and had to move out of the apartment I was living in and I didn't yet know where I would go next. I had been reading Ann Lauterbach's book of selected poems, *If in Time*, and wanted to know how she wrote those poems, how one learned to perceive the world in pieces. How language could become so beautiful.

So I carried a deck of index cards around in my back pocket. The rule was that I had to fill a card and put it at the back of the pile and that I was not permitted to go back and read anything until I'd finished the whole stack. I wrote little journal entries, letters to friends I wouldn't send, lines of poetry. I kept them in sets of twenty-eight, thinking this to be a lunar month, a significant unit of some kind. Arbitrary but functional.

My life in India so far feels like that. Arranged in little clusters of experiences. In Bengaluru, I practise yoga in the morning, wander all afternoon, write a little bit in the early evening, and then eat dinner alone each evening. Empty days are full for me.

From here I am meant to go on to Hyderabad, one of the few places in India that I still have family. Ardeshir will be at the festival there as well, and he has facilitated an introduction for me to various other poets. My uncle and aunt call and ask me to stay with them at their house in Secunderabad, instead of the hotel planned for the festival guests. Their driver will take me each morning, they promise. Normally I like to be by myself, but they are favourites of mine, so I agree.

I've been travelling more than a month and I haven't heard from Ethan. I haven't written either. How long before an ordinary silence turns into something else? I walk from Church Street into the park. It is full of people, sitting and talking, or playing games with balls and frisbees. Occasionally there is a whole family sitting together for a picnic.

The sun is hot and everything in my notebook is cold.

Is Ethan's silence also cold? Or is it warm, as in him giving me space to be here on my own, experience what I will experience?

And then there is the silence of the book, both the book about Michael and this book, the notebook I am keeping during my journeys. What must a book keep silent about?

For some reason I am writing about the end with Michael. And not even why we broke apart, but what happened at the very end.

—

When I thought I was seeing Michael for the last time, I wanted it to be a real goodbye. He knew it was goodbye as well. To prolong the moment, we took the ferry to Staten Island and back.

It was a foggy night, we couldn't see anything. I imagined the statue was emerald in the distance, a light against grey, the fortress in the waves.

Water below slackening to glass and fog.

He slipped on my finger a Turkish puzzle ring made of four bands – gold, white gold, rose gold, and platinum. 'You can't take it off or you won't be able to put it back on again,' he told me.

'Unless I solve the puzzle,' I say.

The statue, the fortress, the light, all fall into darkness.
Soon we will be in open water, clothed in fog, with no marker but memory.

—

At some point I must stop writing the things that stick in my memory and listen instead, listen for things that I have forgotten.

I met Ruman because I had seen his photo on social media. I liked the way he looked and so I clicked. From his profile I learned that we had ten mutual friends and they were friends who I knew from all different cities, all different time periods, all different moments of my life, including college, my organizing career, my life in New York, my life at the college I then taught at. This man and I had been living parallel lives, just barely not managing to intersect. I wrote to him at once. When he wrote back and we started talking, we both realized that we would be in India at the same time.

—

After leaving Varkala to come here, it turns out that I am spending the weekend alone. Ruman has written to say he cannot get away because of family obligations and he will call on me next week.

For the moment, I'm an actor in an abstract landscape, a metascape. As in my favourite plays, when the stage is empty you can actually see.

Nest. Fire all around. A shadow drama. I decide to go to the college of fine arts to look at the paintings. Ruman instructs me how to give the rickshaw drivers directions: 'Tell them it is the big white building next to the fuel station.'

The directions are so ridiculous to me that instead I just ask them to take me to the college of fine arts. None of them knows where it is. I have to get in and out of three rickshaws before I say, 'It is the big white building next to the fuel station,' and the fourth driver knows exactly which building I mean.

Later I find out the reason why there is such a collection of art from around the world here: Svetoslav Roerich, the son of the Russian painter Nicholas Roerich, married the movie star Devika Rani and came here to live. He gave the college a lot of money and all his father's paintings.

And the paintings I see seem to be narrating my life, naming the days in it with flat monochromatic vigour: Yellow day. Blue day.

Lines of water. Each painting a window of some kind.

A painting depicting Sita covered in music, lost in the woods: Michael, after death.

A painting of Radha: on the left side, a beast with the head of a woman reaching through the red colour field; on the right side, lush jungle leaves. Me, waiting to be loved by no one who will ever be able to find me.

In the middle of them, Krishna in a flowered dress playing the flute in front of what seems to be a minaret, its cool lines laced with a frenzied scribble meant to resemble calligraphy. This same scribble appears in the colour field, scratching away the red paint.

I chant the Radha Krishna mantra. It is meant to bring one love. But do I want love? I've left Ethan. I'm already planning how to avoid meeting Rishi. What exactly is it that I want? I chant anyhow:

Keshavi Keshavaradhya Kishori Keshavstuta
Rudra Rupa Rudra Murtih Rudrani Rudra Devta

Around Krishna and Radha in the painting, like another kind of frame, bloom savage red flowers on a black background.

As I look at each painting, I wonder how it would be transformed structurally into forms of fiction. For example, the sculptor and printmaker Krishna Reddy makes these incredibly textured prints with mostly abstract and geometric forms, softened by their multiplicity of layering, given poetic and narrative names: *Maternity. Mother and Son Separate. Praying Woman.*

Is my book about Michael like that? Telling the story of Michael, I have had to leave almost everything out. Maybe because it is the story of endings. Michael is gone. But it is also the story of the ending with Ethan, and Ethan isn't even here for it.

Why do I find it so easy to allow things to recede? Is it my family that taught me to accept being unloved?

But today, here in a strange city, unattended by the friend who called me here, wandering a museum for hours looking at paintings by artists I have never heard of before, I think: *I like being alone.* But not because I don't need another. But I have become accustomed to this feeling, this sadness.

Kamaraj had told me not to leave Varkala. 'Your treatment is not complete,' he said.

'But I've had some,' I bargained with him. 'I'm a little better, right?'

He smiled and nodded, conceding. 'You are a little better.'

Then I see *The Magical Man* by Jatin Das. He has wings but he is bound. A magical man who cannot fly, who looks in two directions at once: toward the past and toward the future, but he himself is suspended in the present. He cannot move. There is no way for him to release himself.

I have come to look at paintings because here I can feel familiar. The architecture of art museums, like the architecture of a bus stop or of a bathroom, seems to be more or less the same no matter where you go in the world. Now, why is that? Why is a room always four right angles and a flat ceiling? Why aren't domestic spaces culturally specific? Why does a kitchen in Paris look the same as a kitchen in Bengaluru? Besides a flourish here or a little visual accent there, they mostly conform. Is it engineering or something else?

Ruman writes later that he wants me to do a reading of my poetry in the city while I am here. I'm not sure about it, but we choose a day.

I feel I am no one's, I belong to no one, I'm nothing, an empty ghost, absent, unclaimed. I look at the lush figures painted by Amrita Sher-Gil, a painter who died at only twenty-eight. I have seen photographs of her. She was glamorous and beautiful and was maybe bisexual and maybe died of peritonitis after a home abortion. Her eyes gleam in the photographs and make me think of Uma Thurman from the film where she played Anaïs Nin's lover June.

I say 'lover' though it is never clear that June and Anaïs were lovers. Reading Nin's diary, it seems obvious that Nin was in love with June, or thought she was, but she never describes physical intimacy, except in a dream. Nin confessed so much else, it does not make sense she would leave this out, and though she wrote many lesbian sex scenes in her for-pay erotica, the relationships between women in her novels and short stories are all sublimated into the emotional, devoid of the physical.

For her part, June Miller had numerous ongoing lesbian relationships, and seemed to have been more queer than straight, for all that her reputation is mostly due to her marriage to Henry Miller. At some point, as reported by Henry to Anaïs, June seemed dismissive of Nin as someone who was slumming with them or experimenting. Nin continued to become enamoured with other women, but none of those relationships approached the intensity of the early one with June.

I look at the painting by Amrita Sher-Gil and think: *Like me in my book about Michael, she flattens detail. She uses one line to imply a whole garment, a leaf or two to mean the whole tree.*

You have to fill in the rest.

—

I am writing the world; it is a tough clot and will not unravel.

Each word serves out a sentence.

Michael is dead.

There is the sound of keys turning in a lock of an apartment down the hall. I am afraid by instinct to turn to look.

A key turning in the lock. Flight.

No, fight.

—

I walked an hour back from the gallery through Cubbon Park. It is sultry, all the families are out, playing games or lounging. Young men wrestle in the grass, laughing. I am sore and hungry but happy.

I am living in breath and body and unable, except through them, to release myself into the formless forms of the universe's multifold energy.

Michael was the reason I stopped eating. He was so thin himself, and I was too, not because of body image but because the summer I finished graduate school I had no work and I was able to scrape by on rent payments, but I had very, very little left over for anything else, and I reasoned that if I were disciplined enough I could save money on food. For weeks I ate grapes and powdered soup and drank green tea and bought the day-old and two-day-old rolls from the bakery around the corner from my apartment.

But the thinner I got, the more attention Michael paid to me. 'You're so handsome,' he would say. 'You are so beautiful!' he exclaimed after not seeing me for a couple weeks, during which time I had dropped just short of ten pounds.

Then after I started being able to eat a little more, I would run every day, four or five miles, to make sure I stayed skinny.

I've always recognized that moment as a hinge point of real danger but I have never been able to properly explain it, even now.

—

I think of it here because every day the hotel sends up a breakfast, either a greasy omelette, cooked Indian-style on high heat so it is hard and crispy, not the fluffy kind one gets at home, or else they send up dosas or spiced potatoes, or puttu. Before breakfast I do an hour of yoga and after I go walking in Cubbon Park.

One morning, unexpectedly, there is a message from Ethan. There is a little green dot next to his name to show me he is online right now. It is late the previous evening for him. We are talking across time.

As if a month hasn't passed, he goes straight for the ordinary: he tells me about the seeds he has planted in the garden, about the different chores around the house he has been doing. He writes, 'How is the book going?'

'It's not going well. I don't know what is supposed to happen in it,' I type back.

'Do the two of them end up together at the end?' he asks, as if it is a book of fiction, though he knows it isn't.

'They don't,' I admit.

'So it's not a love story at all,' he writes back.

'No, it is,' I insist. 'It's about the *way* they loved each other, not the reasons why.'

The three periods flash to show he is answering. 'I guess I don't understand,' he writes.

'What don't you understand?'

'If you don't know the reasons why you love someone, then is it love?'

It bothers me he would say that. 'Love is a *feeling*,' I write.

More dots. He's thinking. 'I guess I don't believe that,' he writes. 'I think love is what you do, not how you feel.'

'Well,' I write then, 'Michael dies at the end. They can't end up together.'

'That's a cheap way to end a book about why two people who love each other don't end up together,' Ethan writes. 'It's too easy. There should be something else. Like, maybe they realize they don't actually love each other.'

Do I love Ethan? Does he love me?

'Maybe that's the tragedy. They were soulmates but they still couldn't be together,' I offer.

'I don't think I believe there is such a thing.'

'I'm not your soulmate?' I venture.

His answer comes back too quickly: 'No.'

Maybe Ethan could write a better book of love than I could. He would write about all those events I'm skipping. The ordinary things, like planting seeds in the garden. All the endless silent meals, washing the dishes afterward and going to bed early, tired from the day.

Maybe Ethan's book would have one of Duras's endings: either the lovers reunite, but only as aged people with a lifetime of separation behind them, or else the book ends at the parting, their parting and the falling of an anonymous bystander into the sea.

Rather than the writing of our earthly lives, I am writing a prose that behaves like water, wind, or fire. Why, always, are books made of rocks instead? All the jagged edges have to fit together perfectly so the structure stays intact and sound enough for a reader to wander inside it without danger. A book that is just a map to something that has already happened, a book in the past tense.

What about a cartography of exploration, a prose that is itself *happening* as the reader engages? What about a book so incendiary it catches fire in your hands?

—

How does sense splinter in sound? I'm exhausted. Every song on the radio makes me think about how I am alone, how I don't have a family. What did my mother think about me in her last days? Is my father thinking about me now?

Our perfect goodbye, the fog-drenched boat journey, was not goodbye. We saw each other again, Michael and I. And we fought, that last time. We ended in hostility. Such a cliché. We fought about something that didn't even matter, about politics and war. And Ethan and I, the last time we saw each other before I came here was ordinary. We lay in bed. He woke and showered, I left. There was no battle, no words of love or regret. Not even a goodbye. I just left.

How long do we all go on pretending things that seem unimportant don't matter and don't still hurt?

My uncle who lives in Hyderabad had been an actor once. His roommate in college was Shyam Benegal, who went on to be an important director in Indian cinema. In the early days, when Benegal was scrambling for financing, he pressed my uncle into service playing bit roles in his films, including, most famously, the patel in a film about village life. By the time I was growing up, my uncle had given up acting and had become a painter. At some point he gave up art altogether and started a business delivering tiffin lunches to workers. I felt some form of kinship with him because he was one of the few people in my family who had made a living as an artist, though I always promised myself that I would never give up art.

Two years ago, I came out to him and he told me that there are no sins against God, only sins against other people, so that my only job was to explain to my parents about being gay, to help them to come to peace with it so they could be happy. His kindness makes me want to go and see them.

There is a cool breeze running down through Cubbon Park; the elevated train runs by across the street, so much quieter than the trains in New York.

I miss New York. I left New York like I have left everything. With no reason. Well, there was a reason. I had to work. *No, because if you stayed you would have transformed*, I scold myself. But I am transforming here. It's harder. Yes, but now I can prove to myself that I don't need anyone else or any place to transform, that I can transform from within. That is a quality shared by butterflies and saints.

—

I'm lost and rent, I rang myself like a bell. I swirl and eddy like water, like breath, like blood. Our bodies are not entities but events, phenomena, temporary coalitions in physical form.

I'm thinking more about the kinds of writing there are, the kinds of art there are – whether fire or water or earth or air. What different arts are made of and what they are for.

Touch: dance, architecture, poetry, and sculpture; each of these are literally made of blood and breath.

Music is an art of the instant; it is received by the ears, is immediate and physical. It elicits embodied responses in the tissues and organs of the body. Its impact lies beyond intellectual responses.

Painting and photography are arts of space and time. Of the mind. They require reflection and contemplation to be experienced and understood.

Cuisine and aromatherapy and perfumery: taste and smell.

Theatre and installation art and performance art: a staging between dance and painting.

Prose. Is prose an art? Or a craft?

⁓

On Thursday Ruman arrives to take me to a meeting of gay Bengalurians. There is a white American transwoman there who has adopted Indian manners and mannerisms. She wears a sari and calls herself Radha and speaks with a particularly Indian English – Inglish? – dialect and accent.

Immediately I criticize myself: Why do I notice and remark on her transness? Does her crossing of gender reflect in some way her adoption of Indian cultural manners and body language?

At any rate, she's taken the bad with the good: during the meeting the men and the only other woman in attendance, a butch lesbian, were all sitting and discussing recent legislation in the Lok Sabha and what the community response should be, while Radha clattered around the small kitchen making and serving the tea. Once more: Why do I comment on the queer woman's butchness? Is it her genderqueerness that allows her to sit with us talking about the news and politics while Radha makes the tea?

Later, on the way to dinner. Ruman tells me more about Radha. She'd come as an exchange student for a semester; she was not then presenting as trans. It was while in India that she decided not to go back home and started transitioning, wearing Indian women's clothing. Being here in India, away from American rigidities of masculinity and femininity, perhaps allowed her to access a greater facility in transitioning.

Though we have our own kinds of rigidities here.

We eat dinner at a small restaurant near the meeting room, and it becomes clear that Radha has no money when she claims to not be hungry. It is the same trick I used to play in graduate school during my broke, starving days, when I didn't want the people I was with to know how poor I was.

So I play a trick back: I order my own food and then claim to not be hungry enough to finish it and offer her half. It's not a fancy restaurant, and the menu, like those of the restaurants in Varkala, has separate sections – English and Indian, only as opposed to the panoply of options the Varkala restaurants offered, reflective of the tourist populations, including French, Swedish, Japanese, and Israeli. Remembering the meals of my childhood, I order baked beans on toast. I give Radha one toast, smothered in beans.

I am being generous but still selfish enough to be annoyed, because the food is very good and I wish I could finish it myself. My annoyance is immediately tempered by the pleasure of realizing I do actually *want* to eat. I feel like I should write to Kamaraj and tell him.

'It's good,' I say instead. 'It's *good*.' The food in my mouth tastes good. She smiles a genuine and kind smile. She eats.

'I don't – ' I start. Why should I explain anything? 'It's not – '

'It's *so* good,' she says, nodding. Does she know? That I don't usually like eating? It doesn't matter much. Here we both are, strangers in bodies we didn't know, but now finding our way.

—

Somehow, even though Ruman organized my reading in only three days, it has been covered in the local paper and there are sixty or seventy people packed into the upstairs room of the Penguin bookstore.

I meet a young man named Krishna at the reading, he goes by Kish, and he tells me about how even though his parents know he is gay they are still trying to arrange a marriage for him. Afterward, we all go to a Chinese restaurant. Kish walks me back to my hotel and we stay up late talking about books and music. He is learning Karnatik-style vocals and so he sings a little for me. I read him more poems.

We meet the next afternoon for lunch. He takes me to a Mangalorean place for fried fish and prawn masala. Then we get in an auto and drive out to the mall where there is a bookstore he wants me to see. All the books are shelved horizontally here, which makes it so much easier to find what you want.

In the auto on the way back, he puts his arm around me and I lean companionably into him. His parents live in the hills and have a coffee plantation. He has always wanted to travel around the world, he tells me. Where do you want to go, I ask him, and he says Thailand and Cambodia and Burma.

That night I write to him, asking him to meet Ruman and me at a bar south of Church Street whose top floor is known as a gay-friendly space. He comes and I feel an instant physical attraction. We sit next to each other and have a whispered conversation, but not about books or music this time: we talk about our days, we talk about ordinary things. We want to be friends who have known each other a long time even though it has only been a day. We both want more intimacy but we don't have time to grow it, so we pretend.

Kish works in a company. He has never been to an art museum nor to the meeting I went to with Ruman. He doesn't think about politics. I try to explain to him why it all matters.

—

Another man comes over to sit with us and talk with Ruman. When Ruman tells him I am a poet, he wants to recite a poem to me but only if I know Hindi. I say I know Urdu but I will try to understand. He recites a line that means something like 'The sky gives itself to the earth as rain.' I ask him what an unfamiliar word means and he gets upset, saying, 'I thought you said you understood Hindi.' I ask him to please recite the rest of the poem anyhow so I can at least hear the sound of it. 'What's the point?' he asks brusquely, and turns back to Ruman.

I open my mouth to say something, but Kish leans over and says, 'Don't listen to him. He doesn't understand.'

Though Kish is trying to be kind, it irritates me. It's *me* who doesn't understand in this case. And the line is beautiful – the sky giving itself down into the earth – and I want to hear more. I have this nagging feeling that I'm sitting next to a real poet, whether he knows it or not, and I'm going to miss the experience. I pluck at his sleeve and he looks back at me with annoyance. I let go.

The moment reminds me of a conversation I once had with Ethan. I was frustrated, angry even, that my work was not receiving attention.

After years of writing and translating, I was still slogging along. Ethan said, 'But are you happy?'

'How can I be happy when the most important thing in my life is undervalued?' I asked.

'Your poetry is not the most important thing about you,' said Ethan. 'Even if you never write again, you would still be an important, valuable person.'

It was the first time I really thought that Ethan and I didn't belong together, that he didn't understand me at all.

'Come,' says Kish. 'Come. Let's go somewhere else.'

He drives me on his motorcycle through the outskirts of the city to a place where there is a gay nightclub called Pink. I ride with my arms around his waist and up his jacket, my hands on his bare skin.

On the way to the nightclub we stop several times by the side of the road because he is hungry to take me. He pulls over to the side of the road, then twists to grab a hold of me, kissing me roughly, deeply, intensely.

The club is incredible. Despite my earlier experiences at the club in Kerala and at the bar across from Church Street, it is overwhelming to be around this many openly gay men, and for the first time I realize what a cosmopolitan city it is: in addition to Indian men from all over the subcontinent, the crowd is very mixed and international, with more Chinese and Black men than I have seen on the streets of the city I have travelled.

'Are you still upset about the poem?' Kish asks me.

I shake my head. Here, with music loud and Kish close to me, it matters less.

'You are my poem,' I say, and he rolls his eyes and takes my hands and pulls me close.

As we dance, someone's mouth comes close to my ear and whispers my name. I pull back from Kish and turn to see a man smiling at me.

'It's you, yes?' he asks. I nod. 'I saw your picture in the paper. You read your poetry at Penguin.'

Kish smiles. 'You're famous,' he says.

It's flabbergasting to me. In America I wander around lonely and dissatisfied, unloved and anonymous, yet in India I have been recognized twice in public places in as many weeks. My poetry readings are covered in the newspaper.

One could get used to it. And also not.

The man follows Kish and me around all evening, wanting to talk to us, wanting me to tell him what he should read and wanting to tell me what I should read. He wants to tell me about his family that is trying to arrange his marriage and to show me the scar he has from an appendectomy he had to have last year. It's an excuse to pull his shirt up and show me his body. I don't mind.

I think about Surya, about the wounds we all carry, the wounds others can see and the wounds they can't, about how sometimes we all want others to know the ways we are broken and sometimes we don't. I think about Radha, who had to come around the world to be able to look into a mirror and see herself the way she always wanted to.

I don't have it in my heart to tell the man to leave us alone, so Kish and I spend all night talking with him and dancing with him. Later, when we leave, we have to say goodbye because there is room on Kish's motorcycle only for me.

⁓

The heaven of Kish's skin on mine as we sleep at my hotel. In the hot night we are naked. We are still sticky with sweat and semen. His cock rests against my hip, and every once in a while, in his sleep, it surges and vibrates. He has the sweetest smile, even in sleep, like a child. His body is thin like Michael's, but unlike Michael, lanky and tall, Kish is small.

We kissed and enjoyed each other's bodies, but he is too large to suck properly and so large that fucking was out of the question, so we spent ourselves by pressing and thrusting against each other and kissing.

—

We lie in each other's arms all morning. I don't want him to release me. But I'm not sure what more there is to talk about when we both wake.

I default to talking to him about the issues I learned of at the meeting the other night with Ruman. I explain to him some of the issues in the Indian parliament right now and the different issues facing gay people in the Indian workforce. Kish listens intently. If he is bored, he doesn't show it.

—

The next time I go to the museum, I get there quickly by giving the rickshaw driver the proper directions the first time around. Radha is there, waiting for me by the gate, her arms crossing and uncrossing. When she sees me, she waves.

'Thanks for meeting me,' she says, as we go into the lobby. I take out my wallet to pay, but Radha is already paying for both of us. I let her. 'There's a painting I wanted to show you,' she says as we walk inside. 'To thank you for sharing your food with me.'

I open my mouth to protest, but she smiles and holds up a hand. I nod.

We walk through the gallery and suddenly I know where she's taking me. *The Magical Man.*

'I love this one,' I say.

'You know it?'

'I was here the other day. He's bound but he's free. He's looking backward and forward.'

'Most people I show it to think he's in trouble,' she says.

'He's not in trouble,' I say. 'He's in a position most people would think is trouble but it isn't to him.'

'To us,' she corrects.

'To us.'

—

I see myself come alive in the sweetness and briefness of these new relationships without any pressure to continue them. I wonder what it would be like if there were more time, if I wasn't always arriving or leaving. But no one has asked me to stay. Radha is one more woman I could be friends with if I stayed longer. Kish is one more man I could imagine the potential of being with but I will not stay with long enough to learn what might be possible.

There are so many languages I have not yet learned.

-6-
VOLCANO

The literary festival in Hyderabad is being held in Taramati Baradari, an ancient complex that has been renovated to hold arts events and performances. In the shadow of the infamous Golconda Fort, the complex was built by one of the sultans of Golconda for his favourite Kuchipudi dancer. Because it was constructed with the cooling technologies of ancient architectural principles, wind is always blowing through, and even when the days outside are hot, it is temperate – even cool – in its halls and galleries.

Hyderabad is made of some of the most ancient rocks in the world, a volcano range that erupted in a chain of massive explosions sixty or seventy million years ago, geologists guess. There are massive smashed boulders, each shard ten times bigger than a house, littered all through the landscape. One theory about the extinction of the dinosaurs is that it began here, whether by an asteroid falling out of the sky or by the chthonic forces of the mountains shearing against each other and shattering.

Ardeshir appears. He gives me the newly published volume of his *Collected Poems*, hand-bound in bright blue canvas covers with gold threaded through. We go into one of the lecture halls to listen to a talk on translation. India is a fascinating place to talk and think about translation because there isn't as much as you would think between Indian languages.

Because so many people are polylingual, often reading four or five different languages, there's less of a need to translate from English or Hindi, for example, or from one Indian language, like Kannada, into another, like Marathi or Odiya. Translations from international languages like Russian or Arabic or Japanese are often done from the English or Hindi versions into Tamil or Telugu or Malayalam, rather than one regional Indian language to another. It's remarkable because, for one example only, there are more people in the world whose first language is Tamil than those whose mother tongue is Italian or German.

Perhaps that is why Ruman's friend at the bar was so impatient with me. I think about Laxmi and imagine that being in India and being able to speak only one Indian language – English – and not others makes me a functional illiterate in this society.

I am captivated by one of the women on the panel. She is sitting at the end and she speaks only a few times, but when she does her voice is lilting, her manner tentative, as if she is not sure of what she says. Yet what she says is poetic and thought-provoking. 'How can one actually translate into any language,' she ventures, 'when one's own language is still so mysterious? Does anyone actually master it?'

'Who is that?' I whisper to Ardeshir, and he practically scoffs. I guess not everyone's a fan.

'That's Meera K. Do you know her?'

Meera Kannadical. Of course I know her, she's practically a legend in American poetry circles, and now I recognize her from the author pictures I've seen, which are – in the manner of those so openly vain about their appearance they must be forgiven – some decades old. She's as glamorous as she ever was, and in the opinion shared by Duras's admirer, I find her even more devastatingly beautiful with age. Her sari is a resplendent and rich blue, with silver embroidery, her dark hair is unbound and shines with amla. Her loose tresses are woven with jasmine flowers. Meera Kannadical, known to those in the know as Meera K, is an Indian-American academic who grew up somewhere in the Midwest but came to Hyderabad, her family's ancestral home, on a sabbatical to research Indian anglophone poetry. Instead of the promised critical book on poetry, she became heavily involved in the protests against corruption in the government and police brutality against the poor and women. Her poetry led to greater awareness of casteism and violence against women, and she dropped out of her doctoral program and never went back to America, staying on instead in Hyderabad and continuing her political work, writing both poetry and prose, and translating local writers.

I stand in line to talk to Meera K though I don't know what I will say to her. There is another man ahead of me who looks like Kish from the back, small and slender, but when he turns to talk to Meera I see he is very different, shy and delicate, with black glossy hair and beard. He talks to her in such low tones that even though I am only a little bit away, I can't hear what he is saying. He is speaking with deliberateness and intention and she is captivated by whatever he is saying. Or maybe she is captivated by *him*. I know I am. She laughs girlishly, resting one hand lightly on his thin shoulder.

I get warm thinking about being looked at the way Meera K is looking at this man right now, straight into his eyes, following everything he is saying. As he leaves, I am briefly torn between following him to wherever he is going and staying to talk to Meera K. My moment of indecision costs me. It is India, after all, and the concept of a queue is tenuous at best. A crowd of people swirl past me and surround Meera K. She casts off her serious expression and lets out another little girlish laugh and begins immediately conversing with the new people who arrive. Two of the women begin speaking with her in French and she answers them in that language, all the while speaking with the rest of the people using a blend of English, Hindi, and the drumming tones of Malayalam that had become so familiar to me during my time in Kerala.

It's a fascinating contradiction of what she had said on the panel, and I find myself just standing and listening rather than trying to inject myself into the conversation. Any question I might have seems less important than witnessing this moment of spontaneous speech and translation.

I'm weak, tired from the heat. Want more water, less food. I sneak off after the opening session and find one of the empty rooms on the far side of the crescent-shaped building to practise yoga undisturbed.

Because my stomach has been so unsettled, I'm fasting today, just taking juice. There's music and a dance performance tonight, but I am feeling tired, and besides, my uncle's driver has to come pick me up and I don't want to be a lot of trouble and make him wait.

A boy of nineteen or twenty arrives in the room where I am practising yoga. 'The sir wants you,' he tells me as I am stretched out in an extended side-angle pose, one arm bound under my thigh and the other reaching behind my back to clasp the opposite hand.

'The sir?' I ask, unclasping and standing up.

'The sir with the white hair,' he clarifies. Ardeshir. 'He says he needs you and you must come.'

I sigh and swallow my annoyance; I buckle my sandals on and collect my satchel and follow the young man to one of the arched alcoves where Ardeshir lounges, smoking a bidi.

'Oh, my friend,' he says dramatically, holding his arms out for me, 'I thought you might be *too busy* with our *esteemed* Meera K!'

I take one hand and wag it, declining to float into his arms as he seems to want.

'So *formal*,' he reproaches, batting those mournful eyes at me. 'And I thought after *Madras* that we were *friends*.'

I thaw immediately. In spite of all his dramatics, we *are* friends. There is some part of me that even loves him. Desperately. His sadness that is all-pervasive: it could easily have been me. It *has* been me. And yet behind that puckish performance of grief is a deep and powerful commitment to live. I am immensely attracted to him even as I simultaneously do not want to become him.

'What's happened, Ardeshir?' I ask, sitting next to him.

'I'm due in *Jaipur*,' he says, as if it were a jail sentence. Jaipur is the one festival I've always wanted to go to but I have never been invited. When I knew I was coming on this trip, I debased myself and wrote to the festival director, a writer from Scotland who has made his home in India for many years, suggesting (truthfully) that I rarely come to India and that since I would be in Chennai and Hyderabad, it would be easy to come up to Jaipur. He did not respond.

I wait for Ardeshir to continue as I am sure he will.

'Oh, it's such a *tamasha*,' he says, stabbing at the air with his bidi. 'Everybody just *clutching* at you. *Please* come with me, you shall be my *chaperone*.'

I notice that the boy who came to summon me is still lingering, twenty or so feet away.

'*Array*, Vivek,' calls out Ardeshir in a wheedling tone. 'Go fetch us some chai.' Vivek dutifully scurries off in the direction of the mess tent.

Varkala already feels like a lifetime ago, how sad. I want to go back. But where do I live and who am I? Ardeshir needs a friend, but so do I.

'I can't go with you,' I say simply. 'I'm staying here in Hyderabad for a few days after the festival – '

'With *Meera*?' he asks, suddenly angry.

'No, not with Meera. I haven't even met her yet.'

'She's a *bitch*,' he says.

'Language, Ardeshir,' I say, laughing. 'We don't use that term.'

He rolls his eyes. 'Oh, we can't say *bitch* in front of the *American*. It *upsets* him. Well, what about *dog-ess*? Is that better?'

I shouldn't laugh at it, but I do.

'Meera K,' he says, gesturing with his arm as if introducing her, 'the *dog-ess*.'

'I'm staying in Hyderabad to visit my family for a few days. And then I don't know. I thought I would stay in India. I'm not sure. I already miss home.' What I'm actually thinking is to turn back around and return to Varkala.

'Very well,' Ardeshir says curtly, stubbing the bidi out and rising. 'You are only the latest in a *line* of beautiful poets who have *abandoned* me at my time of need. Perhaps I shall ask the *dog-ess*.'

He takes my arm and we walk back to the pavilion where the festival is serving chai and snacks. We meet Vivek on the way, hurrying back to us with a hastily put together tray with cups of steaming milky chai and some fried pastries.

'No, behta, bring it back to the *tent*,' Ardeshir says impatiently, as if Vivek ought to have anticipated our return.

We go in and join a large group sitting around one of the tables, talking and drinking chai. Meera K is there, though she is still talking to the two French-speaking women. Perhaps, like Surya's friend Louis, they are from Puducherry. The young man who was talking to Meera K is also there, listening to others talk about the poetry reading that has just happened. I introduce myself to him.

His name is Prasad and he is a schoolteacher from Gujarat who now lives in Mumbai. He came out for the festival, to listen to the poetry in Kannada and Malayalam and Tamil and Telugu since the Hyderabad festival is the only one that is multilingual and includes poetry readings and panels in all these languages as well as in Hindi, Urdu, and English. He wanted to hear the rhythms of languages he neither spoke nor understood. I can relate.

I ask him if he too writes poetry and he is about to respond when Ardeshir wants me to come away to sit with him. I am feeling like I have had enough of Ardeshir for one afternoon, but I ask him to join us instead. Ardeshir smiles benevolently, acting as if he is the one being generous by bestowing us with his presence, and then turns his attention, and not kindly, to Prasad. 'And *who* are *you*?' he demands.

'A person,' Prasad responds evenly, unintimidated.

—

A translator from Kolkata brings an anthology of poetry translated into Bengali; she has done fifteen poems from one of my books. I ask her to read a poem to me and suggest she complete the book. She reads some poems. I do not recognize my rhythms but like the sounds of the language. It does not sound like my poetry. Later, when she has gone, Ardeshir tells me the translations are quite good but that she read them badly.

I think of all the delicious ways I have failed, the madness I squandered. But after Varkala, even this echo of criticism sinks slowly out of sight, feels nearly anachronistic.

I left some shadow there lingering at the beach. I am not afraid to change. I have already changed.

And I wait still – *still* means unmoving and also means connected in some way to the past. I am drawn in any direction toward what's to come. Which means I am unfolding.

This is what the 'southern sky' means to me – to see anew, to be seen anew, to be as the dew suddenly appearing and then disappearing with the morning sun.

I don't feel good about the book about Michael, if it is a book at all. I am not sure if it's ready, musical enough, lyrical enough, anarchic enough. Does it refract, does it scatter the light, does it splinter the tongue of certainty into beautiful Babel?

Why don't I say something real, something difficult, something that would explain why I started loving Michael or why I stopped?

For example, *Michael is the reason I stop eating. I think: if I become thinner he might love me. Michael wanted me to kill myself the way he eventually would.*

'I'm writing a new book,' I find myself telling Prasad and Ardeshir. 'About someone I wanted to love but couldn't.'

But that's not true. I *did* love Michael. It's Michael who wanted to love *me* but couldn't.

'Another book of love by someone who loves too much and cannot ever be loved back in the measure he longs for,' Ardeshir says quietly. Then, with the air of one who has made a decision, he rises with purpose.

'Come!' he instructs. 'Not you,' he says brusquely to Prasad, and takes my arm and leads me off.

Sorry, I mouth over my shoulder to Prasad, who just rolls his eyes and smiles.

'I'll have you back in time for your uncle's driver,' Ardeshir says, leading me out of the complex and hailing a rickshaw, which bears us down the road a little while; we emerge at the foot of the hill upon which sits the Golconda Fort. 'It was Nin's mystical city,' he tells me as we walk through the galleries and begin climbing the rampart to the summit. 'She put it in Mexico, but it was this place she was describing in her novels.'

Nin: that dream of a writer who wove her life into fiction and wove her fiction into life.

'I knew her,' Ardeshir says casually as we arrive on the ramparts at the summit. 'When I was doing my PhD in the States, I wrote her a fan letter and she summoned me to New York and I went. I spent the afternoon in her apartment. I am not sure why but she told me *everything.* Maybe because she knew she would never see me again, but she told me about her two marriages, she told me about all the affairs, *everything*: the one with her analyst, the one with her *father.* I thought I was the luckiest man in the world. Then I never saw her again. I imagine that was *necessary.* Because I *knew* her. Fully. A few weeks later I got this short little note from her, thanking me for coming and saying how nice it was we spent the afternoon talking about Djuna Barnes. *Djuna Barnes?*' He laughed, not kindly.

The terrace overlooking the valley. In the setting sun I can see the hilltop temple overlooking the Taramati Baradari.

'That temple is where Taramati would go in the evenings and sing. Because of the acoustics of the valley, he would be here on the ramparts of Golconda, and he would hear her as if she were next to him. So he fell in love with her without ever seeing her face. Only by hearing her.' Ardeshir pauses. Then, in that same decisive voice he used in the tent, he says, 'Wait right here.' And he scurries off down the staircase around the corner.

I turn to look over the valley, at all the shattered mountains, the Hussain Sagar sparkling blue, the stretching arms of the Old City, the Second City, the hills.

'Can you hear me?' I hear Ardeshir's voice in my ear. I spin, alarmed. He is nowhere on the terrace. 'Can you hear me? Look this way. Look out toward the galleries.'

I look back down the series of esplanades we climbed, and there, hundreds of yards away and below in one of the first galleries, is Ardeshir, waving his arms. He disappears briefly into the shadows and I hear his voice again in the air around me.

'The engineers used ancient acoustic technology to amplify the voice. This was the alarm system of the fort. The sentries spoke to each other. Speak to me.'

'I can hear you,' I find myself shouting, and Ardeshir laughs.

'You don't have to scream,' he replies in a normal tone. 'I can hear you. I hear you.'

⁓

Thursday evening. I have locked myself in the guest bedroom of my uncle's apartment. Why did I even try to pray in a language that doesn't fit my mouth? Certainly no one can stand between you and god.

What happened was this:

My uncle asked if he could talk to me. After a long time of weaving about and talking around me and talking around my relationship to my family, he told me bluntly that being gay was not natural and that some other external person – or the Devil – had put it into my heart and that I had to leave Ethan and get away from him.

I felt sick to my stomach. He said that I was selfish to be causing my father pain. Then he said that the reason my mother had died – of a sudden aneurysm – was my fault, that her worry over me had overwhelmed her. When he said that, in spite of myself, I started crying. He said he was sorry to hurt me but he would rather hurt me than hurt my father.

He said he would battle to keep me safe. He asked me if I was afraid that Ethan would hurt me if I tried to leave. I couldn't believe the words coming out of his mouth. As if Ethan would ever physically hurt me.

I felt like I was in a reality where everyone had gone mad. For a moment I was frightened. I am still frightened, sitting here late in the night, inventing crazy scenarios, worried about what could happen to me here, what could happen to Ethan, how we could be hurt, made to suffer.

It makes me want to get away from all of this, get back to my own life, my own people. My aunt and uncle didn't write me back in the beginning because they didn't want me to come, I am now realizing.

Then they realized Ethan wasn't with me and asked me to come.

How is this different from my own parents, who never wanted Ethan in their house? Even at my mother's funeral, which I begged Ethan to come to, people in my family were upset with me for asking him. In spite of all this, I still try to continue to work toward closeness with my family.

My uncle said I was selfish for not sacrificing my own desires for the well-being of my parents.

He said maybe god was preventing me from loving a woman but that god never forced me to love a man.

I trembled in my skin. Where I should have been enraged I turned instead into a small, soft thing. I felt myself dying.

But I was so numb as he spoke to me, I just kept thinking to myself: *How do I get through this? Should I just stand up and leave? But I don't know where to go. And I don't know how to call a cab and I don't have a phone that works in India.* My entrapment was real.

My uncle went on and on about how he gave up his movie career and his art career for his family, and I should be able to do the same. I told him that he shouldn't have given up those things. He said that sexuality is powerful, and when people are magnetic they owe it to the people around them to be more careful. He told me I should be celibate rather than gay.

I felt like I was in a film or a play or a novel instead of real life. But if it were happening to someone else, if it were just a made-up story, it was not a very funny one. How had my uncle changed so much from the last time I came?

I thought again of just standing up and leaving immediately, then I thought of sneaking out and leaving all my things, then of trying to leave early and moving to a hotel. Eventually my uncle said he was going out. He said that unless I was planning to go out, he would padlock the door behind him so no one would break in. My blood ran cold and I told him he needn't bother, but he laughed it off, saying it was best to padlock the door as it is not safe to leave the apartment unlocked.

Now in my room alone, I look frantically at the books I bought at the festival, trying to find one by a writer who lives in Hyderabad: perhaps they, like me, wouldn't be staying at the festival. I can't find one – everyone has travelled here from other cities.

Then I realize, there is one writer who lives here in Hyderabad, who would not be staying in a hotel room: Meera K.

I'm not sure what inspires my bravery, but I email the festival organizer for her contact information, which he sends me. I intend to send Meera K the briefest email, saying I would like to meet her before leaving for the north.

But how do I explain it? To someone I need to rescue me? Someone who has made a career of rescuing people in far more dire circumstances than mine? Though now, locked in my room, late at night, afraid to go to sleep, I feel in dire enough circumstances.

I keep it simple. I write, 'Can we meet for lunch tomorrow? I am staying with my family but it is untenable now, I cannot stay here anymore.'

Though it is late at night and I do not expect to hear from her until the morning, a message flashes: 'Send the address. My driver will come for you immediately.'

She knows.

I send the address and then I type back, 'No, I will stay here until the morning. I have to say goodbye to them.'

She writes, 'My driver will come for you at eleven in the morning. Bring all your suitcases with you. Just say you are visiting me for a day or two.'

I take a breath. She knows. I have a safe harbour. Now to get through the night. I hear them moving in the apartment. I hear my uncle on the phone. He is talking to someone in English. 'I explained it to him,' he is saying. 'I do not know if he understands. Give him time.' Who is on the other line? My father?

I take a breath. If Kish were here, he could spirit me away on his motorcycle. And Surya, who imagines I am so strong to be living openly as a gay man, what would he say now? He would know why I am hiding here in my room. He has done the same thing, I am sure of it. I think of

Prasad calmly answering Ardeshir's nakedly hostile 'Who are *you*?' by saying, serenely, 'A person.'

As strong as I have always thought I am, I feel so vulnerable right now.

In spite of myself, in spite of the time and space I thought I needed, in spite of how strained things are between us right now, there's only one person I wish were with me. He would be so enraged by all of this. He would not understand why I am staying in this house one more minute.

I open my computer and send one more message. An email, to Ethan: 'I'm at my uncle's house but I'm leaving tomorrow and I'm not coming back. Please come to India. I want to be here with you.' I am about to press Send, then I add: 'I need you.'

Knowing there is a nearly twelve-hour time difference, I add, 'I won't see your message until seven or eight hours from now when I wake up.'

I have to try to sleep or I will be awake all night. I've locked the door with the deadbolt. I feel alienated and alone.

My uncle subjected me to every form of emotional blackmail he could devise, including saying I am like a pedophile who might believe his own sexual inclinations are 'also natural.'

I am pierced. And too numb to bring myself to react in anger or leave the house. I can only plan ahead: it is four in the morning now. Meera K's driver is coming in seven hours. I want to take my whole self and soul with me. I can't sleep and I don't want to have my room light be seen from beyond the door, so I write by the street lamp.

I can only imagine the terror in the hearts of those people who cannot leave their families. Must they succumb to this awful pressure? What about women who have even less freedom of movement and less economic access necessary to claim freedom for oneself?

I must save myself.

And who put him up to this? Who was that on the phone?

Should all of this have happened fifteen years ago, I would have been lost, I would have succumbed, and then I would have died. I never would have written any books, I would have withered, and then I would have disappeared.

I see now that it is not the light of the street after all that has kept me with enough illumination to write but the light of the apartments across the street. As it gets later and they go to bed, my own light gets less and less.

Soon I sit in the dark writing on the page, not seeing what I write but knowing it is there.

—

In the morning, while the cook prepares breakfast, my uncle jokes with my aunt, saying, 'Our nephew will never come and stay with us again.' They both know how much I am hurt, that he went too far, that I've shut down emotionally as my only way of responding to it.

He isn't my blood relative, but he and my father grew up in the same village and were best friends from their childhood. I don't know what is left of my relationship with my father, but whatever there is, I want to try to save it, if I can. I want to make it to eleven o'clock with dignity and then leave with Meera K's driver without any big confrontation.

My phone vibrates with a text from Ethan. No message, just details of a flight: 'Arriving Thursday morning 11:30am, Delhi.'

I thought we would at least talk first to make travel arrangements, and so at first I am annoyed, but then I see the time stamp on his message. He sent it almost immediately after I sent my message. He must have bought a ticket right away, the first one he could find. No questions at all.

Something warm grows inside where a lonely place had been. The clammy chill I had been feeling on my skin begins to melt. Ethan is coming.

So, this little black journal book in which I am writing holds the sun and breath and joy of Varkala, the loneliness and bliss of body of Bengaluru, and now this, the poverty and doom of Hyderabad. Maybe a novel could be written of these three places, a short one, a real one, maybe realer than the long-ago memories I am trying to archive about Michael, about a love that died long ago.

Rather than being about the death of love, a book about how a person finds love in the present moment.

And what does it mean that Ethan is coming? Will we find our way to each other? Who will it be that appears? And who is the man, half-ruined, he will find?

'We are having a guest,' my aunt announced then. The guest in question is both the last person I would expect and the one person in my family I would perhaps most want to see. A wayward aunt, Sarah Khala, clad in a sky-blue wrap, her hair startling and silver. I haven't seen her in thirty years. She is more beautiful and radiant than I remember her.

She is a cousin of my mother's and we all loved her as children because she was the only member of our family who wasn't Muslim: at some point in her youth, she converted to Catholicism and in the years since then she became Pentecostal. The adults in my family were always silent somehow when she was around, like she had an illness they were worried we might catch. A deeply devout Christian, especially one who now travels the world on evangelical missions, may seem an unlikely ally for the only gay person – so far as I know – in a Muslim family, and yet, and yet.

My uncle and aunt embrace her like old friends. This is not how I remember her being treated before. What do they think is going to happen here? Maybe that my aunt will also condemn me, bring me into line somehow? But to me she is magical. We talked about Palestine, Romania, Cape Town, all places she has been on her travels for the Church.

Sarah Khala reads grace over our dosa and idli, while my uncle and aunt sit reverently, their hands folded in front of them like Christians, praying for one of my cousins and my other cousin's husband, both of whom have been diagnosed with cancer. Sarah Khala also prays for my aunt, who has her own frailties and aliments, in words eloquent and passionate.

Sarah Khala begins to regale us with tales of a recent trip to Botswana, but as much as it interests me, all I want to do is talk to Ethan, whisper to him in the dark.

I think of a letter to my father I might write but that I would not send: 'So now I am brokenhearted, alone, no friends, no kind harbour, no supporters who see me and the kindness that breathes in this tenderest of hearts.'

Add those texts to my book about Michael, more texts never to be sent to the people they are addressed to.

This morning was the kite festival, where the children use kites with glass-coated strings to try to cut another's string and win their kite. The skies fill with kites of all colours. The newspaper tells the story of a child who fell from the roof of one of the neighbourhood buildings and perished.

I tell my uncle and aunt that I am leaving and they seem unsurprised. In the light of day and with Sarah Khala present, the danger I'd felt all night evaporates. When Meera K's driver arrives, I am already out on the street with my suitcase, and I'm surprised to see that Meera K is in the car too. As soon as I am in the car, she is on my side, condemning my family for hurting me, for summoning me with the sole purpose of trying to bring me back into the fold by inflicting damage. She understands immediately what has happened without me saying a word.

As we drive to Jubilee Hills, on the other side of Hussain Sagar, where she lives, I fill her in on everything that happened, including the arrival of Sarah Khala that morning.

After an initial quick barrage of updates, we settle into easy conversation, talking about poetry, the festival, living in Hyderabad. We drive past the new neighbourhoods called Cyberabad, after all the tech industry that has moved in, and up into the hills. We pass a house shaped like a giant gemstone that Meera K tells me is a landmark for the drivers coming to her house. I smile, thinking of the fuel station in Bengaluru, which is the only way anyone can find some of the greatest paintings in the world.

We drive up a winding road into the hills all the way to the end. Meera K's house is the last house before a great empty lot where the Tollywood crews always come to film, she says.

I meet an ancient woman she calls Ma but who she tells me is not her mother, and another woman about her age she calls Bee, who seems to be a servant. While Bee finishes cooking lunch, Meera K takes me into the garden. We walk and she tells me which trees are which: the papaya, the pomegranate, the banana, the moringa. Lunch is chawwal, dhal, and drumsticks from the moringa. There's spicy nimbu pickle, as always.

'You can stay,' says Meera K. 'We'll send you in a taxi to the airport in the morning.'

We read poetry to each other into the evening, including a book of Ardeshir's that Meera K has on the shelf, one of his early books. I marvel at the photograph on the back cover. He is devastatingly handsome, with large lash-fringed eyes, not yet grown mournful, his mouth resting easily in a smile of seduction, not spite.

'He's different now,' Meera K says, as if knowing what I am thinking. 'People have treated him so badly. All he ever wanted was to be accepted by others, by his family and friends, by other writers. No one ever took him seriously, no one was kind to him. They didn't include him in the anthologies, they wouldn't invite him to the festivals. He left, you know, for many years; he lived in Iran, in Palestine, in Egypt. He only came back when he was old and needed to be close.'

She doesn't need to reassure me. Regardless of everything, I like Ardeshir. Not just because his poetry is beautiful, but because something of that grievously wounded spirit feels familiar. And there's something admirable about the contentious and prickly way he faces down a world that has always been hostile to him.

'You're not friends?'

'We were once,' she says. 'But a castle can only have one queen!' She laughs. I laugh too.

'How did you decide … ?' I begin, not sure what I am going to ask her. 'To stay in India?'

That's not it. I know why she decided to stay. 'You stayed because what you had to do here felt more important than anything there was to do back home.'

'I don't know that the States ever really felt like home,' she says. 'I grew up in Ohio, you know. It was only once I went to college that I felt I was meeting people who did things other than what I had always been taught. But it's true. How could I stay in New York and lecture on Wordsworth when the women here were in such danger?'

But that's still not it.

'I think what I really want to know is: How did you decide to still be you? The saris, the glamour, all of it.'

She laughs again. 'I'm not what you expect.' I shake my head. 'Not the poet who wrote "The Orange Sellers' Protest,"' mentioning the one poem of hers everyone seems to know.

'Well,' I say, gesturing to her ruby-lacquered nails, glittering with gold rings.

She pauses and glances at her reflection in the mirror on the wall. 'I don't know,' she says slowly. 'I've lived the only life I could. I tried to have as much integrity as possible in public and in private. I tried to allow myself pleasure and rage. I could not turn my back upon the beauty that does exist in the world and I suppose I myself want to be beautiful as well. Ardeshir and I are the same, you know. Maybe that is why we can't be friends. We each had to conquer the world around us just to be able to live in it a little.'

'And all the languages? French, English, Hindi, Malayalam...?'

'And Arabic and Italian,' she completes, laughing. 'I don't know. I'm different in every one. A different version of Meera. I'm quite clever in

French! In Arabic I'm rebellious and political. But in Malayalam I am mostly an obedient daughter.'

I know something about that.

⁓

Even though I am perfectly safe at Meera K's house, I still bolt my door shut. I lie in bed, terrified by how powerless I felt last night and how completely I gave up my authority over myself to my family by agreeing to stay with them. What if they had taken me somewhere? I had no way of getting free, no language to escape with, no way of getting a car or knowing where to go or what to do.

And then as I drift into fitful sleep I hear that voice again, across a great distance, across years and centuries perhaps, the voice of some ancestor of mine who maybe lived here in this place, who passed these streets, a voice rusty with grief and regret:

'Can you hear me? Can you hear me?'

And so, across years and miles into the night, to whomever might be listening in the past or in the present or in the future, I whisper: 'I can hear you. I hear you.'

-7-
SEED EAR

It's three when Meera knocks on the door to wake me so I can be on time to catch my six o'clock plane to Delhi to meet Ethan. I slept only twice all night, each time for only a minute or two. One of the other women, Bee I think, is rustling around the kitchen. Meera has called a driver for me. While we wait, she puts on a record. Expecting something Indian, I am surprised when the light piano of Beethoven's 'Moonlight Sonata' comes out of the speakers.

'It's an evening raga rather than a morning one,' she says, 'but I've always preferred it in the dark hours of morning.'

'I'm sorry I woke the whole house up,' I say, but she waves her hand dismissively.

'These are my hours ordinarily,' she says. 'I find it the right time to write poetry.'

'You still write poetry,' I say, a current of electricity running through me.

'I never stopped,' she says simply. 'I don't publish much anymore. I don't think I want to. The whole scene – it *bothers* me. I would rather do my political work and teach my classes.' She looks at me with a questioning look. 'Does it upset you?'

'Upset me? That you don't publish? Why would it upset me?'

She shrugs then, an impish smile replacing the almost troubled look she wore just a minute ago. 'It's no matter,' she says gaily. 'None at all.'

Bee appears then, with an omelette for me, a plate of buttered toast for Meera K, and two cups of steaming, fragrant chai.

My eyes go wide at my first sip.

'It's Bee's special recipe,' Meera K says. 'She's from Baluchistan. She crushes cardamom pods into the pan of milk.'

We both sip then, savouring the steeped brew. How is that I can talk so easily with Meera K, or Ardeshir, whom I had barely met before becoming fast friends, but I could not speak to my uncle, could not make him understand. He believed me deceived by the devil. But it was I who deceived myself into believing that people can transcend the prison walls they have built around their perceptions.

He told me I was selfish and the worst out of all my cousins, and what would they think of me if they knew. I am crushed that someone so lovely, eccentric, artistic, and lovable could be so convinced of his own rightness, completely unable to see the human creature sitting right in front of him. If my uncle, an actor who became a painter, jovial and eccentric, could not see past the scripture he holds fast to, then who could?

Although maybe that is the real reason why he could go no further in art.

It's a foolish line of thought, I suppose – great art has always been created by flawed humans – but at the moment it gives me some comfort.

The car comes. I leave Meera K there in the dark. She'd lifted the needle and reset it to listen to the sonata again. In the car to the airport, I think to myself that my uncle's tumbling down from his place in my mind only endears me to my own father. My father's refusal to speak or engage is kinder and more considerate of my feelings than my uncle's blackmail and manipulations. My father isn't trying to 'save' me. Deep underneath his sadness and silence is his fundamental respect for other people and their rights.

It was not my father on the other end of the phone line that night. I'm certain of it. Tears well up in my eyes. 'How many years?' I whisper in the darkness of the cab's interior, as if my father could hear me. 'Can I call you now?'

I emailed Ethan in the middle of the night, didn't I? Asking him to come. Maybe it would be as simple to reach out to my father. I think of all the letters I never sent to Michael, all the calls I never made to my mother.

Time passes until it doesn't. And then it stops and you are suspended in that moment, the moment of the death of the other person, held there forever.

—

After I get off the plane in Delhi, I take a taxi to the international terminal and wait with the rest of the crowds for arriving passengers. There are more people than I could have imagined. America seems empty in retrospect after the crowds of India. How on earth will I ever see Ethan, I worry.

I remember a trip to India that I took at sixteen. My parents were reluctant to let me travel alone but I assured them that I would be fine. My father had written out *pages* of instructions for me about the airport, which counters to go to when and with what information. He had arranged for a family friend who lived in Bombay – as it was then called – to meet me at the international terminal and accompany me to the domestic terminal, where I would fly to Hyderabad and stay with my uncle and aunt for the summer.

When I arrived, I followed all my father's careful instructions, but the aunt who was meant to meet me was not at the meeting place when I emerged from customs. Sick to my stomach, with no local money and very little street smarts, I sat in one of the chairs and just *waited*. Waited for what, I don't know. Meanwhile, back in America, my father had heard from my aunt that I had not been where she went to meet me and that she couldn't find me. In a panic, he resorted to the only method of crisis management he could think of: he started making dua and promising donations to various religious causes if I should be found.

What happened was, at the first moment of my own panic, when I finally realized my aunt wasn't coming, and while I tried to figure out what to do, a man sat down next to me. He asked me what was wrong and I told him. He had two friends with him, a young man and woman, but they didn't say anything. He told me that my flight to Hyderabad would be leaving from another terminal and I needed to take a cab. I said I didn't have any money. He gave me fifty rupees and took me to the cabs and put me in one.

My father, when he heard I was safe in Hyderabad, said his prayers had been answered and that it must have been the angel Khidr who came down in human form to assist me. My mother later told me that he had been beside himself with worry.

Maybe it was easy for him to feel tenderly about me in my absence. I never could explain who the young man was who helped me or why.

The crowd swirls around me. It is impossible to truly explain the sensation of India to a person who has not been there. How first pink then blue then orange or silver bloom. The smell of bodies, of chai, fried food, and jasmine flowers woven through thick braids glistening with amla oil. Sounds of cars, and voices calling, the wind and animals and song.

In the night in Hyderabad, feeling like a person burning alive, the person I reached for was Ethan. Even when it felt like things were ending. And what does it mean that he came, that he received my message and knew immediately the nature of the crisis was such that there was no time to waste, none at all.

There aren't many people in the world like that for me, I suppose. I've moved so many times in my life that all the friends I'm closest to I knew for only short periods and they are scattered all over the country and world. Few are the people who live close and listen hard. Even Michael is an echo from another life, less a ruin of love than remnants of the ruin.

But Ethan has been the constant. There all through the years, even when we were barely speaking, even when he would spend a day in the same room as me and not say a word. But here I am, still, quivering with anticipation, straining through the voluminous and billowing crowd, trying to catch one sight of him.

And then, as if thinking about him summons him, he materializes out of the crowd. He looks tired, his hair is messy. In spite of myself, in spite of how lonely I sometimes feel with him, I tremble to see him. I needed him and he came. What was it he wrote to me? 'Love is what you do, not what you feel?'

And how is it I managed to find him in this crowd? How is it things happen properly in India at all? Somehow, with the thousands of people and overabundance of stimuli, every atom just seems to careen in the right direction for the world to continue its work.

Then Ethan is in front of me. Then my arms are around him. He is holding his bag and so holds me with only one arm. 'Put your bag down,' I say. 'I want to feel you.'

He puts his bag down. He holds me close. We stay like that for a long time. I just want to feel him against me. It is not that he burns my loneliness away. Sometimes in his silence it makes me feel *more* lonely to be in a room with him. But at least he knows me.

Since he's come all this way, I ask Ethan what, besides the monuments and temples, does he want to see in India? He is a farmer and so he wants to go out to Dehra Dun, where there is a research farm focusing on heritage seeds and reviving traditional Indian agricultural techniques, ones that do not use corporate seeds and agribusiness pesticides. I don't know what I will do on a farm for a week, but for the moment, as long as I am with him, I don't mind. We reserve train tickets.

We have the whole day in Delhi before getting on a late-night train, so we book a car and driver at the airport, and the only place I can think to take him is Chandni Chowk. The whole street is a market and it runs near the Jama Masjid down to a Jain bird hospital, a Tibetan market, and finally what's left of the Red Fort in Delhi. I have not been much of a Muslim, but I know enough to tell Ethan to wear long pants, and it's a good thing, because the other European tourists at the masjid, who have come in shorts and sleeveless shirts, both men and women, are made to wear low jelbabs covered with a bright tropical floral pattern. The fort here is neither as extensive nor as impressive as the Red Fort in Agra, but Ethan's never seen anything like it. We wander its grounds and then go through the bird hospital, wondering at the care given to even the smallest creatures, their little bones practically a living metaphor for the fragility of life itself. On our way back to the car we stop by the Tibetan market to pick up blankets for us each to use as wraps against the cutting cold of the Indian winter.

Chandni Chowk is not much to look at but is governed by its sounds and smells. We eat chaat and idli sambar at Haldiram's, and drink it with fresh lime soda. I order the sweet lime soda and Ethan chooses the salty, but it turns out to be black salt, which he hates, so we switch. The papri chaat is divine: sweet and salty both at the same time, with pomegranate seeds, spices, and yogurt.

'There are so many people,' Ethan murmurs, 'I almost feel seasick.'

It's true for most Westerners: that first day in the street in India is overwhelming, and Ethan's metaphor of seasickness is apt. The people come in waves, endless waves, the sensation of them, their bodies, the heat, the perfume of jasmine and agarbhati, the smell of sweat and amla, it's all dizzying.

With Ethan beside me, though we barely speak, I feel the ghost of Michael and sickness of Hyderabad slipping away into the crowds. I reach down and take Ethan's hand as we walk into the streets of Paharganj, the car cruising along beside us. The driver did not understand why I wanted to walk and I had to argue with him for nearly ten minutes before he allowed it. Ethan stiffens suddenly at my hand's touch and looks at me, shocked.

'It's okay,' I say, tightening my grip. 'Look.' And I gesture around us. He looks and notices we are not the only men holding hands.

'I don't understand,' he says.

'It's just different. Men touch each other here. They hold hands, they don't have the same kind of personal space as we do.'

We watch as we walk, and Ethan points out two younger men, maybe twenty, one sitting on his scooter and the other leaning against his chest, smoking. The man on the scooter has both of his arms around the other one.

'It's kind of hot,' Ethan says with a crooked smile. Oh, I've missed that smile.

I am alive. Perhaps I have gone through fire, but I am alive.

—

The driver is right. After only about fifteen minutes we climb back into the car, grateful and exhausted. We spend the rest of the day on a whirlwind tour, going to the Qutab Minar, the Baha'i temple, and the Gandhi Smriti, where Mahatma Gandhi was killed. My favourite place is the mausoleum of the emperor Humayun. It resembles the more famous Taj Mahal but is made of red sandstone rather than white marble so somehow feels more of the earth, less heavenly, more ordinary. Which I like. Feeling ordinary myself.

By the time we get there, it is early evening, the air is cooling, and the Maghrib call to prayer rises into the air from many different mosques in the vicinity, each a little off-sync with the others so it sounds like a chorus of voices.

For some reason the dozens of voices make me think about two talks I am to give when I return to the States. One is called 'God at the Gate' and the other is called 'Ethos, Pathos, Logos.' 'God at the gate' sounds like 'barbarians at the gate,' so it is an acknowledgement of the barbarism of spirituality, not just religion. Any thought of 'god' means it is something outside of you, not inside as breath, which is what 'spirit' means.

I think about 'ethos, pathos, logos' and wonder if a proper talk on the subject would have to locate who the 'speaker' of a poem is, which means you know 'who' a person is. But I don't. Perhaps instead I should attempt a narrative of India: I could write about each different city trying to capture something of its energy and essence in the way I write about it: first Chennai, then Varkala, Bengaluru, Hyderabad, Delhi, Dehra Dun, and then our return.

But how to write the truth of how the body feels in sexual ecstasy in an essay about god? Anyhow, I don't want people to know that much about me. I don't want to tell about my problems with Ethan, about my family, about Michael and his death. It's all too personal. I envy my friends who are novelists. They can turn things in their life into fiction, or maybe they don't turn it into fiction at all, maybe they just do it like those French writers do that I love so much, just change some names here and there and call it fiction, as if it is made up, as if it happened to someone else. Maybe instead of giving a talk, I should just read from the diary I am keeping, including the shreds about Michael.

But even if I did dare it – transcribing my diary and putting the word *fiction* on the cover – I would still have to add little details to make it feel a 'realistic' story. An irony.

Or I could choose little pieces of it and make them into stories. I could tell the story of the new year, how I sat on the beach with the bickering couple, watching the new year draw in, the dark ocean roaring, my skin singing in the breeze. Or about how now I am here in India with Ethan, wishing he could love me with more romantic passion, wishing that I needed less.

After years of torturing and killing myself in spirit, I resolved to live my life bravely and fully the only way I could. I promised to breathe, I promised to never again have fear. And remarkably, even when I thought I might be harmed or kidnapped or killed, I did not panic in Hyderabad, not really, I had guts all the way through.

What does it say about me? Stupid or heroic?

After an all-night train, we arrive in the very early morning in Dehra Dun and take a car out through the night fog for what seems like another hour before we arrive at the institute. I can see nothing in the dark. We sit on the veranda for a while before the caretaker arrives, close to daybreak, and immediately makes us hot, milky, sweet tea to keep us warm while he opens the office and gets out the register book.

We meet the skeleton crew here. There is Chris, a carpenter from Seattle. There are two women from New York City, Gail and Betty, who is a physician; they are donating money to the institute and have brought some equipment and supplies with them. Then there is Nathalie from Rennes, who has been here five months already and speaks passing Hindi in a charming French accent. There are others, they tell me, but they are away on a trip to Rishikesh and come back on Tuesday.

We worked in the morning, helping to prepare turmeric for market by cleaning the dirt off and cutting the roots into smaller pieces, and then ate lunch and rested in the hot afternoon. I practised yoga for the first time in four days. My uncle from Hyderabad calls every day, ten or twelve times a day from his own cellphone, ten or twelve times a day from my aunt's cellphone. I do not answer the calls.

I worked hard to build a life, be true to my spirit and so tender in my house. Why should I tremble before such bullying? Why should I even answer it?

I find myself folded up into the shape of a man who doesn't exist anymore – an earlier version of me who never fathomed ever coming out to his family. I lived that way for decades before I finally did, and when I did, it seemed to me to be incidental, but not to my parents or my family.

And Ethan and I haven't talked. About what drove me to India without him, about what caused me to reach out and ask him to join me. About why he dropped everything and came. About what we're doing here. Somehow it's easier that everything's unspoken.

—

The others have come from Rishikesh; Donny and Linda, a schoolteacher and biologist, whom Ethan knows from the urban farming community back home, are among them. They are here with a project around seed-saving. We take a walk through a tulsi thicket along an abandoned riverbed and then through the village before making our way back to the institute.

Gail has had a run-in with Linda about the kind of research Linda is doing at the institute. I'm not clear on the details, it is something about foundations back home and who is providing the funding and whether or not Linda is interacting with the scientists at the institute the right way. I've never had a head for politics, so while Ethan tries to help Donny and Linda write an email in response to Gail, I take a walk. There's nowhere to walk and I'm nervous to leave the compound on my own, so I walk up and down the planted furrows in the field. I do not know what they are growing, but on the far side I discover a man sitting in a work area in front of another building. He has paint out and is in the process of painting metal lanterns a dark green. I imagine also for sale, but I don't know. He sees me and gestures toward the brushes and paints, thinking I have come there to help him with his task.

I suppose I have. I take a brush. I sit.

The painting is easy work, and afternoon draws into evening without my noticing.

All the workers sleep together in a big room on narrow cots. It is hard to have Ethan so close but not beside me. It is so cold that they have given us heavy jackets and wool hats to borrow in the evenings. We all sleep in our clothes, jacket and socks and shoes still on. I even wear my wool hat to bed. I lie awake and listen to Ethan breathing. My uncle continues to call.

I repeat to myself that verse from the Quran: 'O Merciful Beneficent One, save me from the mischief-makers among djinn and men.'

The sun warms us in the morning. The heating system for the water is sun-powered, so unless you wait until the afternoon to bathe, it is still very cold. That first morning I get brave enough to bathe from the bucket and it is ice-cold and bracing.

Later I do yoga. There are no mats, so I have to practise on bare concrete. It has something to do with the conflict between Gail and Donny and Linda, which I still do not understand – in my defence, Donny and Linda are equally confused. At any rate, Gail took the yoga mats and cut them into pieces to cover the lab's bare counters. Ethan and I help Linda and Donny remove them and resanitize the wooden counters.

⁓

One day, we drive into the market in Dehra Dun to run errands. I am looking forward to seeing the central city square with the big clock tower that is described in Ruskin Bond's novel *The Room on the Roof*. It's there, but the vibrant square described in the novel it is not. It's a major thoroughfare, clogged with cars, bicycles, rickshaws, animals, and people. Off the main square, there is a strange bombed-out street, the front half of the buildings just sheared off as if by a laser or sorcery or some huge mechanical device. They are working on widening the street, I am told.

I remember being fascinated by buildings and construction, all the equations needed to make a bridge go across water. The world is made of math.

Why isn't a book made so easily? Instead you stumble forward in the dark, adding a line, a sentence, a chapter – sometimes they don't even make sense. But to tell the truth, I prefer a book like that, one that is messy and in which the story is barely legible. I'd rather that than one tightly constructed and edited, with a gun in the first act that goes off by the third. Is that how our actual life is lived? Or is it strange and unfocused, with barely any purpose discernible?

—

I rose earlier than everyone else this morning and walked back and forth again along the furrows of crops from the farm to the seed bank three or four times. I still have no real title for my new book, nothing that hasn't been heard before. I don't want to feel like I am erasing Michael. *Effacement* isn't right, though I am thinking of him less and less as the days go by, writing in the book less and less. *A Riff? A Score?*

And it's a ragged book of threads, it has no edges, no beginning and no end. I watch Chris repair a hinge on the door to the kitchen. How envious I am of those writers who know how to turn the screws and make a good cabinet. A shining book. A perfect one. So perfect it's dead.

I remember still the day I was drifting in and out of sleep. I felt a shadow on my face. I was half-conscious but aware that Michael was over me, his mouth just barely brushing my mouth. He did not kiss me, like he couldn't bear it or couldn't dare it.

And me? Still lost in the middle of the ocean, treading water, waiting for some key to turn, some tumbler in the lock to fall into place and door to swing open.

A field of yellow flowers, Ethan is resting in the room.

I have to think deeply about architecture, invention, the way I make a claim for myself: *Michael: An Effacement.* Our life in New York, the fear I had of getting emotionally close or vulnerable with anyone – it's me who was 'effacing.' Why should Michael, even after death, suffer the fate?

Though is an effacement always a death? Being here in the country, away from language, away from people, has made me lost but also happy. Who am I here? No one knows me.

This morning, sitting and waiting for the car that was going to take us into the city, leaning against Ethan, his arm around me, his rain-cool skin, his sun-filled smile.

Measure of blue, measure of sky. Michael: a Fathom, a blue fathom, sky. Michael: Saint Fallen. Michael: Confessions of. Michael: a Sketch. A Lore.

─

Each day we eat the same thing – rice and dhal with popped amaranth – for breakfast, lunch, and dinner. Sometimes at dinner, there is a little pickle to go with it. After dinner, in the cold evenings, we all sit around one of the long tables and play a game that Nathalie teaches us, called Werewolf. Someone among us is a beast who devours the rest. Someone among us catches a quick glimpse.

It's me, I think silently, wishing to warn the rest of them. *I am the one who will take your faces and names and write them into a book. I am the one who will devour you. I have done it to Michael and I will do it to you.*

Ethan asks me if he can read the book. If he is surprised by how few scrawled pages there are, and how sparse each page is, he does not betray it. I hand him maybe thirty pages, *Michael: ~~A Novel: An Effacement~~* scribbled ambitiously on the first page.

He reads. I look over his shoulder to see what he is reading. What parts he is getting to.

He comes to the page very near the end where I finally learn how Michael feels about me, the feelings he won't share with me. He gets to the part where I say:

He did not kiss me, like he couldn't bear it or couldn't dare it.

And where I continued:

I did not want to move, I did not want him to know I was half-waking. I wanted him to leave his mouth there. That vibrating space, the moment of his lips on my lips.

'He did love you,' Ethan says quietly, 'even if he didn't know why or how.'

'I'm sorry?'

'Michael. He loved you.'

'You mean the narrator,' I say. 'Of the novel.'

'Is that what I mean?' Ethan asks.

I look down at my hands.

'He loved you,' Ethan repeats again, this time more gently. 'He didn't know how to show you, but I think he did love you.'

'Maybe. Maybe he didn't. I am not sure what love is now.'

Ethan says casually, like he's just pulling the phrase out of the air, 'You should call your book *Michael: A Romance.*'

'Why "romance"?'

'Because in a romance the feeling is more important than the actual lived lives. Passion is more important than experience. The thought of love is more important than actual love. You never have to actually agree what it is about the other person that makes it love. That's why a romance has to end when the two people finally get together. It can only tell the beginning. A romance isn't a love story.'

———

In the used bookstore in Dehra Dun I find not a book by Ruskin Bond but a small blue book containing the short stories of Aamer Hussein; they are like music, little poems. I sit on the sidewalk reading. There is a Bodhi tree overhead shedding its leaves.

My own silence is muted by all the actual writing – and this life I describe here, is it real? More or less real because it's been written down?

Maybe when I am again in Kerala before the sun and the sea and having my body worked on, I will hear some sounds. The thing now is that I want to immerse myself in the liquid of poetry itself. I don't know what the shape is supposed to look like.

And so what if I haven't seen Michael in so long. Maybe it is time that makes a book, not language. Adil Jussawalla wrote a book after thirty-five years. Eleanor Lerman wrote a book after twenty-five years, Marie Ponsot also. Robert Duncan after fifteen.

I want to write a book not only about the places I have been through but a book about yoga – a book about salvation, breath, the body, *my* body – yoga, god, and age. A book like every other one it sometimes feels like I have been writing my entire life.

In either case, I will live. I have lost my will to prove something –
that I love god, that I know something, that I am not stupid, banal, or
ugly. How haunted I have been by these forms of weird hatred, how
deeply inside I planted those seeds.

A significant feeling: realizing my body was mine.

Yes, it is true I am leaving behind a way of thinking, all my thoughts
of death. It's me that's dying, the parts I love: the savage despair, the
gruelling relentless feeling that's haunted me.

I can become light as I grow older, grow toward the sun, know that
child power and joy again, know that spirit of breath and ease, that
immense feeling of knowledge, wisdom, kindness, generosity, purity,
magic, bliss – everything is going to fall away.

I too am going to follow and fall.

And me with nothing inside. Trying to let breath go through. Can I
go back to my ordinary life and know myself now?

And how should I write down the lessons, the ones that I am going
to carry back to the cold country, the place I call home?

———

At night, cold and hungry, I dream: more memories, I imagine the
stream of golden oil trickling down:

Kish riding away on his motorcycle, the black helmet adorned with
red flames.

Now I homeward spill.

It came to me once by the river's edge.

Michael's fingers, cupping my jaw.

Pouring water over me.

On the radio, César Franck, Symphony in D.

Anyhow, in the end there were years of silence between Michael and me. I left New York. Michael stayed.

We had our goodbye when I knew I was moving. We took the ferry and had our farewell. So I could go into my exile as if it were forever. I knew even if I came back to New York I wouldn't see him.

Then, some years later, I was in the city for an event and he must have learned about it somehow, because he came with his new partner, a woman my size and with my build and haircut.

I liked her and I didn't.

We couldn't talk about feelings so we talked about the war that we both, even then, in early 2001, felt was coming.

And we fought because I believed we would be able to stop the war, and Michael and his new partner, Britta, felt we wouldn't. I wanted to be optimistic about the abilities and commitments of the activists I knew, and he dismissed my feelings, saying I should read a book called *Empire* by Hardt and Negri.

Somehow his appearing with Britta felt to me like a violence. All my feelings about him changed as soon as I saw her with him.

He meant us to have an ordinary end. One that undid the fog-drenched ferry ride into the night. It made us ordinary. Not almost-lovers. Not really even friends anymore.

Then the buildings fell, or were knocked down, and we all lived in a different kind of world.

The romance ended.

-8-
WATER SIGN

I'd been so happy in Varkala that I wanted to bring Ethan there. It feels like the intersection between us. Sun and water and people for me, silence and empty hours for him. We fly into Kochi and plan to go south and rent a houseboat in Alleppey that will take us through the backwaters to Kollam, and from there will go to Varkala. But first there is a day wandering the old town of Cochin. The streets are narrow, but the trees are huge so mostly we are walking in the shade. It's one of the ancient cities of India, as is Kollam, so I find myself squinting and trying to imagine myself back in time five hundred years when the Portuguese were here or a thousand years when Roman ships and Arab ships sailed to this port.

Ethan is fascinated by the Chinese fishing nets, and we both want to go to the old synagogue in the Jewish neighbourhood, called Jew Town, which in American English borders on the offensive. I notice while trying to read the morning papers that Indian English really is a different language. The words are all the same, but the turns of expression are completely different, some grammatical constructions as well, and though they don't do it as much here in the south as in either Hyderabad or Delhi, many speakers pepper their English with

Hindi or Urdu, so even when you think you are speaking the same language, you aren't.

The synagogue is larger than we'd expected, but not expansive. The community of Jewish people in India, outside of two villages in Andhra Pradesh, is mostly centred here in Kerala, and it's small. I've spent so much time in places of worship on this trip – Hindu temples, churches, mosques, synagogues – but none that really moved me. In every place God seemed more like an idea than something moving in the world I can see and feel. I suppose that is what 'belief' is.

The woman giving us the tour explains what happened to the Jews of India. They left. They went to Israel after the founding of that state.

'Of the approximately twenty thousand Jews who were here in India then, only about five hundred remained. Now there are only about two hundred Jewish people in Kerala, about fifty of them in this city.'

'Lonely,' I say. 'But why trade one exile for another?'

'What do you mean?' Ethan asks.

'Most of the Jews in India are Sephardic and came here in the late fifteenth century when the Christians were taking Spain. India was home for centuries.'

'Maybe it wasn't,' he says. 'Maybe they didn't have a home.'

'Maybe I'm a little Jewish too.'

He shakes his head.

'I mean it. I don't have a home. Maybe it's more a state of mind than a set of beliefs.'

'I'm pretty sure it's a set of beliefs,' he says. And then, more quietly, 'You have a home.'

Do I? And where? I wonder what he means and I wonder if I will ask him. But he doesn't say any more and I don't ask and the moment passes.

Alleppey, where many of the houseboats depart from, is a few hours south of Kochi, on a bumpy, single-lane road. Unlike most roads I have been on in India, including in the city centres, which are shared by cars, auto rickshaws, bicycles, pedestrians, and even animals, this particular road seems to be reserved for cars only, though this doesn't make it any easier to navigate. I feel like I felt in Chennai, driving through the jungles around Auroville, wondering if I was going to find my friend Susan on the other side.

It's like that now, with Ethan, travelling toward we don't know what, haunted by the memory of Michael, and all of what is unspoken between us.

'It was fun being on the farm with you,' I say, which doesn't even feel like an untruth.

'Yes,' says Ethan, but nothing else.

He is comfortable in silence and I am tired of talking, so I turn and look out the window, but it only makes me motion sick. The only thing to do is close my eyes as if I am sleeping, even though I cannot sleep.

⏤

We board one of the smaller houseboats, which nonetheless has a closed-off bedroom for the two of us, a kitchen area at the stern, and a large common area open to the sides. Both the room and the floor are coiled coir fibre, rough enough for me to do yoga poses on, while Ethan lounges with his book. One of the men steers from the front, and once we clear the channel and enter into the wider waterways, he lets Ethan take over the steering. Ethan sits up at the wheel, relaxing in shorts, his shirt shucked as soon as we leave the dock.

I sit back in the shade, watching his back, the sun glittering off the water. I take out my notebook and turn to the last page. I stare at what I've written there: *his lips on my lips.*

Now I know that I have to write the ending part, the part where he and Britta came to New York, the ending after the ending, the undoing of the fog-filled night. I cannot. I close the book.

That night Ethan and I cannot hold each other as it is too hot. We are worried about being intimate because the three men all sleep right outside the door. One stays awake and the other two sleep in shifts, one on the floor of the kitchen and the other in the hallway outside our door.

We spend a day and a night on the water, and by the time we arrive in Kollam I feel restless to set foot on land again but unsure about who I am, who I am leaving the boat or adrift on the water.

—

When we arrive in Varkala, we find a hotel farther north on the cliff from where I stayed last time, farther away from the stairs down to the beach toward the church I did not on my previous trip enter. As it happens, on the way we pass the tailor's shop where I had been measured for shirts.

After we drop our things off at the hotel, I take Ethan immediately down to the beach. By the time we climb down the stone steps, we are both ready for refreshment in the ocean. The water is so warm, the town is quiet and empty, so different than it was over Christmas and even last month. It does feel like the end of a journey. It will take some time before I feel like I belong somewhere again.

I go into the same river twice.

The manager at our hotel is attracted to Ethan and so will speak only to him, treating me with brusqueness, even hostility. I don't mind, but Ethan says we should move. The hotel is farther away than I'd thought from everything and there are so many that are closer, so I agree. We pack everything back up and tell the manager we are leaving. He is offended. He stares reproachfully at me as he processes our checkout. Ethan is enjoying the attention, and so, in a way, am I. I like having something other people want.

We walk down the cliff with our suitcases. 'I like it when a journey has an interruption,' I say. 'Even though we're in the same place. I think every book has a rupture in it too, a subsumed other book.'

'Why?' Ethan wants to know.

'Maybe because you don't know what the book is about until you write it. You have an experience in your life, but it isn't real until you transmute it. Sometimes the rupture is a formal device that structures the whole book, like what Cather does in *The Professor's House*, and sometimes it is more like an invisible seam that is only seen by the writer themself.'

'What's the rupture here then?' Ethan asks. 'What is the rupture in your book about Michael?'

'You,' I say.

⁓

The days disappear one after another, I can't even remember on what day we arrived. At about six in the morning, full dark, the roar of the ocean striking the rocks usually wakes me. I leave Ethan sleeping under the mosquito net and walk out the door to the staircase. I pass the banana tree, its dark flower opening. I walk across the scrubby courtyard of our new hotel out to the walkway, just now coming alive with fishermen bringing their night catches up the cliff to the restaurants and markets. The workers in the restaurants stirring to prepare for breakfast.

Even though it has only been a few weeks since I was here, it feels like a totally new place. One day I take Ethan back to the yoga class on the roof, but Kamaraj says Christine and her boyfriend have gone up to Goa. We are all just tourists in the end, even if a town this small makes you feel like you could make a home in it.

Ethan and I spend the mornings lounging and reading at one of the cafés, and then go down to the beach after lunch. Once the sun grows very long and approaches the western horizon, we climb back up the hundred and eight steps to the cliff to have Ayurvedic treatments at Kamaraj's centre, and then we eat and then we sleep. Even though it is hot, Ethan pulls me close against his body to sleep. I can't sleep but I don't care. I want him to hold me.

My ticket is out of Mumbai in a week and so Ethan booked his ticket from Mumbai as well, though he can't get on the same flight as me. He leaves the evening before me. I will have an extra day.

Varkala is not yet awake. The wind off the ocean keeps it so much cooler than in Kochi. I walk a little down the cliff path to a café that is open early for the returning fishermen. I sit and look over the ocean. The waiter brings me hot ginger lemon honey. It's how everyone starts the day. Some people are leaving, dragging their bags down the path to the helipad, which doubles as a pickup place for the auto rickshaws and the taxi cabs taking people to Kollam or Trivandrum.

What are we doing here, Ethan and I? What am I doing in India in the first place? It's been months since my arrival, and I'm no closer to an answer, even though my departure looms. I have no plan, just to think and wander. I have found myself with new horizons and I'm antsy to turn the page on the book I'm writing about Michael, the book of love and death. This whole time I feel like an entirely new set of imaginary pages has been coalescing under my fingers, my next book, so cheerfully unwritten, just waiting, quite patiently too.

I decide my new book is going to be about Ayyappan, the god born of two men, and the eighteen steps up his temple that a woman took, a book about gender and genre, my Western life, my two lives, my sex-switching like Tiresias back and forth, back and forth, for the sake of prophecy. About the woman Saraswati but the goddess as well, about the stones of Hyderabad and the waters of Kerala – still a poet of water am I, but of fire too now on account of the transformation of yogic energy in my body.

Ethan explains as we sip our tea that the scheme of my book should follow the path of my trip, that it matches the four elements.

I say: 'How?'

He explains:

Chennai: Earth – Mahabalipuram, the waters receding to reveal the temples eroded but still standing on the ocean floor.

Hyderabad and Bengaluru: Fire, in which others tried to destroy me but in which I myself was reborn.

Delhi: Air, in which I flew to meet Ethan, and the days in Dehra Dun we spent.

Kerala: Water, where we lay still and drifted.

How often I console myself for not being beautiful, taller, stronger, by retreating into my talent and gift in poetry. It contains an assumption: that it is compensation to me for being plain and small. For never feeling fully like a man but not a woman either. I am nothing. My wounds are so deep inside as to be undetectable, but they begin at the surface. All you need to do is brush the surface and they leap howling forth.

—

We recline comfortably at the Chill Out Lounge, on divans arranged in a half square, facing out toward the paths that lead away from the cliff to the village. Ethan is trying to blow a tune on a ney flute he bought from a vendor on the cliff. An old man, bald with a big white beard, wearing a dingy lungi and hauling a sack of plastic bags, begs for money at the orange fence. I give him ten rupees to the bar owner's displeasure. 'Don't!' he hisses at me as I hand over the flimsy note. I tell the old man in what Hindi I can manage, 'It is my father who is giving this to you.'

The old man, seeming not to understand what I've said, smiles and nods and waves the money at me. The owner clucks his tongue irritably.

—

I remember the shirts I ordered the last time I was here. Though I had given the tailor my address and money to post them back to America, it is easier now to go to the tailor's and pick up my shirts: one pink, one green, one yellow.

I'm assembling myself, recutting, laying sparely open, a flower, petalled, such a dumbstruck thing.

—

In my reading I am caught between new translations of Lalla and the poems of Kamala Das, two women from opposite sides of the continent and from thousands of years apart who spoke the truth of their bodies and their bodies' experiences as close as they could tell it, though a thousand years apart and so wildly different.

I ran on the beach this morning while Ethan meditated. I bowed to the warm and wonderful surf.

I really did feel in danger in Hyderabad. I felt clearly how our bodies can so easily not belong to us, especially when they are claimed by the family, the tribe, the nation.

My family truly feels that I have damaged them just by claiming basic personhood, the privilege of my own life and body.

And here in India it seems like the price for that is complete rejection from the polity. That is why back home, last spring, I had to spend money I didn't have to buy a house and property; it put me into debt I will never get out of as long as I live, but it doesn't matter because it gave me the sanity to continue to bear my exclusion.

—

It is the morning of our last day in Varkala before going to Mumbai.

'What will happen to us when we go home?' I want to ask Ethan but I do not. We have been travelling on two parallel tracks for a long time. We are friends, we live together, we love each other, and yet I feel alone.

'Who is that?' Ethan says with wonder, looking at someone past my shoulder, out of my field of vision.

I twist to see who he is looking at and I know immediately which person he has spotted. It is a slim man with coal-black hair and skin nearly as dark, with a brilliant blue lungi around his waist, tied in the Keralan style – folded in half and tucked a second time so the thighs and knees are exposed. The man walks, swinging his arms easily, his shoulders wide though bony, his waist so slender the lungi must be knotted twice so it will stay up.

It's not until he's nearly twenty feet away that I see who it is. Surya.

'He's beautiful,' Ethan says, and then because I want to please Ethan, because I want him to know that I too am beautiful, that people find me beautiful, I wave my hand.

'Surya!' I call.

Surya's face bursts out in a radiant smile when he sees me.

'You have come back,' he says, approaching the table.

I stand up – is it too much? – and throw my arms around him. He is surprised but does not pull back. He puts his hands on my back and turns to kiss my cheek. I kiss his cheek.

'We were about to go into the water,' I tell him.

We finish our breakfast and go down to beach and then I wander out in the water to watch the fishing boats, their weathered hulls peeling blue paint, while Ethan and Surya talk, staying in the shallow water, closer to shore. Once or twice I look back and see Ethan touch Surya's shoulder as they talk. Then Surya is leaning toward Ethan, whispering in his ear. Ethan nods.

He gestures to me. I wade back toward them. 'We're going to go back to Surya's guest house. Come.'

We climb up to the cliff and then walk, the three of us, arm in arm, nothing to remark upon in India. Surya and Ethan are joking with each other, I am quiet. I am enjoying being the quiet one. I am enjoying Ethan taking the lead and directing us, deciding we are going to go with Surya, taking charge of the conversation, keeping it going, keeping us comfortable.

Somewhere inside me as we walk I feel like I can relax, I can stop wandering. Wondering.

Ethan kisses both of us deeply, first Surya and then me. I am surprised and aroused by his ardour, knowing somehow it is due to the presence of Surya.

Ethan presses himself down into Surya and Surya moans a little in pleasure. So do I. I know that feeling. Of Ethan pressing himself down into me. Of feeling the air rush from me. Of being scared but wanting more.

Surya wriggles a little. I bend down close to his ear. 'Do you want Ethan to do more?'

He looks at me, his eyes a little afraid.

'Are you not sure?'

He shakes his head.

'You're not sure.'

'I am sure,' he says weakly. 'I want more.'

'But you're afraid?'

Surya's eyes fill with tears.

'Do you want us to stop?'

He slowly shakes his head.

'Do you mean no?' I asked him.

'I don't want you to stop,' he says, crying now. 'Please don't stop.'

'What do you want us to do?' I ask him.

He looks at me then, unsure.

'Tell me,' I say, stroking his hair.

He bites his lip and moans a little because Ethan has put his mouth between Surya's legs.

'Do you like that?' I ask him.

He nods.

'Do you want to do that to one of us?'

He nods frenziedly and I tap Ethan's shoulder and pull him up. Ethan looks from me to Surya.

'Who do you want to do that to?' I ask Surya gently. 'You can do what you want.'

With another little moan, Surya dives down on Ethan, pulling Ethan's hips to his mouth. Ethan's eyes close and he shudders as Surya gulps and slurps at him. I stroke Ethan's cheek. Ethan pulls me to him and puts his tongue in my mouth.

We stay for a long time like that, Ethan kissing me, his pelvis rocking gently against Surya's face, Surya licking and sucking and gulping, his hands still clutching Ethan's hips.

I lean down to Surya. 'Do you want Ethan to enter inside you?' I ask him. He nods again, biting his lip, still crying. I kiss him and touch his tears, while Ethan pulls him up and presses up against him. 'It's okay,' I say.

'Yes,' he says. 'Yes. It's okay.'

Ethan is very gentle, moving slowly. He pulls Surya toward him, lifting his legs up. 'Rest your leg on my shoulder,' he says.

I hand Ethan a condom and try to ease away, but Ethan pulls me back firmly against Surya's and his bodies. I feel their rhythms against my pelvis. I get hard.

Surya bucks up in alarm then. 'It's okay,' I say. 'He can stop. Do you want him to stop?'

Surya looks at me, then at Ethan, then back at me.

'It's enough,' I tell Ethan, 'he's had enough.'

While Ethan is slowly pulling out of Surya, Surya shudders and he releases himself against his stomach with a little cry. Ethan smiles and strokes his cheek. I lean over, wiping Surya's forehead and stroking his hair. He is panting. He smiles and grabs my wrist with one hand and reaches for Ethan with the other.

I move to get out from under Ethan's arm, but he tightens his grip.

'Not yet,' he says, peeling off the condom and reaching for another. 'Your turn.'

The sun goes down on our pleasures, which continue into the night.

—

Morning. We leave Surya to go to Mumbai. I give Surya all the rupees I have left, not very much in U.S. dollars but enough to help him out for a few weeks. On a whim, I give Surya a scrap of paper with the name 'Suraj' written on it, followed by the name of the hotel he works at. We say goodbye.

We sit on the plane, Ethan writing in his journal. I take out the pages on Michael. I turn to the next page. I cannot focus on the past anymore.

Surya's face. Aditi sipping gin. Ardeshir's mournful sigh. Meera K writing, 'I will send my driver for you at once.' My email to Ethan. His email back, saying nothing but giving flight information. Finding each other in the ocean of breath. Wandering amid monuments to the dead.

And then toward the mountains, in a place books and seeds take root. And then adrift. To where?

I've been gone from home for months. I read and wrote and tried to hold my life together.

Tried to be a human even though I had no place, no one, and no occupation in which I served.

Is a person alive or just a functioning part of the lived experience of the entire world? Which is the real thing?

The sculptures of Mahabalipuram: poetry in stone.

By the time I arrived in Kerala I was ready for transformation. First a few days in the weirdly empty hotel and then I began my Ayurvedic treatment with Kamaraj.

My body and spirit responded in the light of the ocean.

From there I went to Bengaluru and back to a normal life of reading and writing. I was lonely but met Kish.

Time in Hyderabad both lovely and poisonous.

I went to Delhi and met Ethan. And then Dehra Dun. Again to Varkala.

All of this while trying to write of Michael. All of this I did from this place of lack.

To learn the limits of myself and not fear the surrender of matter.

All the moments before and between and since.

I cannot hold them, I cannot remember them, I see them once, I let them go.

-9-
INDIA GATE

In Mumbai, we book a room at a hotel in Colaba not far from the India Gate, which marked the arrival of the king to his empire and from which now depart the ferries to Elephanta Island.

The hotel is small and must cater specifically to Arab travellers as the lobby and hallways are full of men and women in long robes, the men in white, the women in black. As we leave our suitcases with the bellhop, we pass a woman sitting at a breakfast table, berating the waiter and shaking a piece of toast in the air.

'What is she saying?' Ethan asks me.

My Arabic isn't great, but I get the gist. 'Something about the butter on the bread. It's white so she thinks it's spoiled.'

Ethan glances back. 'It must be margarine. That's what it looks like if you make it fresh.'

Ethan, holder of arcane secrets. I flush.

We pass out into the hot winter air and make for the Gate, packing onto one of the boats with a crowd of tourists, families, and pilgrims. The island is home to a massive cave temple with a Shivalingam and a statue of the Trimurti I want to see. Unlike the statuary in the south at Mahabalipuram, these stoneworks are in ruins, having been defaced and damaged over the centuries of Portuguese and then British occupation of the place once called Bombay – *bom bai* being Portuguese for the wide and beautiful bay between the peninsular old city and the mainland: Elephanta lies just off the mainland coast.

Floating over the water on the journey across the bay, I press against Ethan. He pulls me close.

Then he asks me. 'Why did you ask me to come to India?'

I don't answer. Or rather I answer with another question. 'Why did you drop everything and come?'

Ethan doesn't answer either. He buries his face in my hair and breathes in deep.

Neither of us speak.

We sit like that – the children screaming and playing around us, the birds wheeling down, hoping for crumbs thrown in the water by passengers and pilgrims – for a long time.

———

From the ferry landing there is a wide staircase, lined with stalls and stands and merchants and hawkers, leading up to the crown of the hill where the temples are. As we climb, I point things out. Ganesh. Shiva. Pan-roasted corn. Jalebi. Parvati. India is a profusion, excessive. I've tried to write about it time and again, in poetry, in fiction, in essay, but one can never really capture it because it lies beyond mere description in words. It is sensual, experiential. It must be heard, smelled, touched, and tasted.

No book can hold it. No words express it.

I remember an argument I once had about colour with a friend. 'Orange and pink and turquoise don't match,' she had said. 'In India they do,' was my unironic retort.

The cave itself is a great relief from the hot climb. We enter the dark recess of the central chamber buttressed by ancient pillars. Though other groups around us are loud and rowdy, I fall into an immediate silence. No matter what I might believe, I nonetheless feel the pure ancientness of this place, which has been hallowed for a long time – millennia even. I gesture to the right, where the Shivalingam resides in another alcove.

We pause in front of it. In the dark I reach over and cup Ethan's crotch. 'It's Shiva's dick,' I whisper irreverently, 'source of all power in the world.'

Ethan starts getting hard. He smirks.

'Do you love me?' I say in the dark.

'What? Where does that question come from?' My hand is still on his crotch.

'I don't know. I just want to know.'

It's a question without an answer and we both know it. 'I came here,' Ethan says, with a tone of having provided the answer.

It's *not* an answer, but I let it go.

———

That evening we've made plans to meet Ardeshir, who has returned home from his travels, for dinner. I want him to meet Ethan but I am also a little apprehensive. I wonder if he will behave.

'Don't tell Ardeshir that I'm going to visit Prasad's school tomorrow,' I tell Ethan. 'He can be touchy.'

I needn't have prepared Ethan. Ardeshir is on his best – which is to say worst – behaviour. As soon as we arrive at the restaurant, his eyes light up. 'Ah, the famous *Ethan*,' he declaims, sizing Ethan up and down.

'I feel like I should ask him to put my clothes back on,' Ethan mutters out the side of his mouth to me.

'Ardeshir, this is Ethan,' I say.

'Such a *sturdy item*,' purrs Ardeshir, 'though I'm sure you will assure me that he *also* has a *soul*.'

'He does,' Ethan says amiably.

Ardeshir sniffs, drawing himself up for what I by now know will be his coup de grace. 'Well, I don't *believe* in the *soul*, only the *asshole*.'

Ethan and I burst out laughing as Ardeshir smiles wickedly and leads us inside.

—

We've eaten well, talked about everything and nothing – as the best dinners often pass – when the topic of our purpose in Mumbai finally comes up.

'What brings you to *BOM*-bay?' Ardeshir asks, emphasizing the first syllable.

'I thought it was Mumbai now,' says Ethan.

Ardeshir scoffs, waving a hand dismissively. 'These *Hindutva* people are rewriting all of history. Was this a Portuguese city or not?'

'Well, I'm flying out tomorrow night,' Ethan says casually, avoiding the argument. 'We couldn't get on the same flight, but it's good enough.'

'And you?' Ardeshir inquires.

'I leave the next evening. But I'm spending my last day writing up my notes,' I hastily add, not wanting to stir up Ardeshir's temper by mentioning Prasad.

'On your *book*,' Ardeshir says, nodding. 'About *love*. What do you think, Ethan? Is there any such thing as *love*?'

'No,' Ethan says bluntly. 'I'm not sure there is.'

Ardeshir fixes his gaze upon him. 'A *realist*. Hardly what I expected of the partner of *this* one,' he says, stabbing a finger at me.

'I just don't think there's such a thing as a "soulmate,"' says Ethan.

'There's that word again,' I mutter.

'No,' agrees Ardeshir. 'No such thing as a "soulmate."'

'But,' Ethan says, his turn to grin, 'nothing wrong with an "assholemate."'

'What's romance anyways,' Ardeshir says. 'It's not for gay people. We don't have big romances like in the films.'

'We could,' I protest. 'Why not? It might not look like Shah Rukh and Kajol in *Kabhi Khushi Kabhie Gham*, but it could – '

'It *might*,' interrupts Ardeshir. 'After all, you *know* what they say about Shah Rukh!'

I'm confused. 'No. What do they say?'

Ardeshir leans forward conspiratorially and casts an exaggerated look over each shoulder, pretending to make sure no one is eavesdropping, and then quips venomously, '*Kabhi* pussy *kabhie* bum.'

―

After we pay, we stand outside saying our goodbyes. Ardeshir makes a big show of hugging Ethan close, but it is after Ethan goes to call the car that Ardeshir takes a tight hold of me, and I feel a tremor of emotion shudder through his thin body.

'Don't forget me,' he says in my ear. 'And don't be angry with me. I am not at all the man I used to be when I had both hope and love.'

I hug him back tightly. 'I'll come back and see you,' I say to him.

'Stay,' he says, with feeling. 'Just *stay*. Accept that position at the university that Santosh offered you and just stay in India.'

'I can't,' I say. 'I have to go back. I don't know. To finish things with Ethan, however they go.'

Ardeshir pulls back, his haggard and vulnerable face hardening again into his habitual sardonic expression. 'I thought things with Ethan were already finished.'

—

Ethan and I spend the morning at Prasad's school, visiting classes, and I give a reading. Later the young students of the Radio Club interview me.

At lunch we eat Parsi food and drink masala soda and have jackfruit ice cream for dessert.

In the afternoon we go to the Haji Ali Dargah, where there is qawwali singing. The dargah itself is out in the shallow waters of the harbour. There is a long causeway that leads to it. We walk under the hot sun.

'So much of this trip has been travelling to get somewhere else,' Ethan says.

A journey that is itself a journey.

'I asked you to come because I thought my uncle was going to kidnap me,' I say, answering his much earlier question. 'I knew I wasn't in physical danger anymore, but my body didn't. I feel at home with you. I feel safe when you're near. Even if … ' I pause. I do not finish.

We walk on.

Ethan decides to answer also. 'I came because you asked me to. Because it's been a long time since you asked me something, and by the sound of your message I felt it was really important. You called me and I came.'

The singing is heard from a ways off. By the time we get to the dargah, the sound itself fills the air. It makes us nearly delirious.

The dargah is here because a man named Ali was lost at sea on his way to the Hajj. His body vanished into the depths and his family mourned him. Then when the pilgrims from that year's Hajj were returning, Haji Ali's body washed ashore – at the point from which he had embarked. Even though he never actually made the Hajj, everyone called him Haji in honour of the miracle.

Journeys always bring you back, even if you aren't the same.

—

I stand outside the hotel with Ethan. His car has come, he has his bags. We are holding each other's hands.

I am trying to think about how to say goodbye when the man from the front desk comes out waving the bill.

'It's all right,' I say. 'Only my friend is leaving now. I am staying another night.'

'You must pay now,' he insists.

I release Ethan's hands and turn to the man, who is still gesticulating. 'No. Just give me five minutes to say goodbye to my friend. He is leaving for the airport but I am staying.'

'You pay now,' he insists. 'Pay now.' I am not sure he understands English.

'Just go,' says Ethan softly.

'I can't,' I say, turning back to him. 'I want to talk to you.'

'Now, you have to pay now,' the man says, getting even more heated.

'Just WAIT!' I shout at the man. Ethan flinches. The man waves the bill in my face again.

'You pay now,' he insists.

'Jesus,' I mutter. 'Just wait one minute for me,' I beg Ethan, and gesture the man back inside the hotel. I walk behind him, shaking with anger. I give him my card and sign the bill and throw it all at him before returning to Ethan, who is standing there at the car, waiting.

'This is not how I wanted to say goodbye,' I say.

'I know,' he says.

'So what happens now?' I ask.

Ethan shrugs. 'I go home.'

'And *then* what happens?'

'You come home.'

—

Prasad came and took me in a cab back to the Parsi restaurant for chicken and wheatberry pulao and vegetarian dhansak. Then we walked back to Colaba and had coffee at a bookstore café.

Ethan must be over Kuwait by now.

'So it is your last night in India,' he says. 'What did you learn?'

'About myself or about India? Or about my book?'

He shrugs. I'm not sure if he means that it doesn't matter which question I answer or whether he means that any answer is not really that important.

'I don't know if I have managed to tell the truth of the relationship. I'm not sure if I captured the atmosphere of life as I was living it at the time. And I don't know how to end it. I didn't finish it. Maybe there is no ending. Though you would think – '

'Show me,' he says.

For the second time in a week I rummage in my satchel. This time I slide two manuscripts across the table. The first is the spiral notebook about Michael, the abandoned book, with my scrawl across the cover: *Michael: ~~A Novel. An Effacement.~~ A Romance.*

The other is the diary I have been keeping this whole time. He looks at the title page of the spiral notebook.

'Which is it?' he asks.

'I don't know. I think it's both. All three.'

He reads. The traffic becomes a drone. He finishes the notebook on Michael and starts reading the diary. Birds wheel in the sky. An hour passes. Then two. I look at my watch. I should have left for the airport by now.

'You don't know how to end it because you don't know what happens at the end.'

'With Michael?' I ask. 'I do know. He dies. I don't even find out about it until much later because we lost touch. It's a terrible ending.'

'But what if it isn't really Michael's story?' he asks. 'What if it's Ethan's?'

I feel like I have been punched in the stomach.

'Then I *really* don't know how it ends,' I say.

He slides the books back across the table to me. 'What if it isn't his story either? What if it's Ardeshir's? What if it's Surya's? Or Kish's?'

I flush. My skin comes alive with memories.

'What if it's *Louis's*?' he presses on. 'What if it's *mine*?'

Birds call.

'What if it ends like this?'

Kazim Ali was born in the United Kingdom and grew up in Jenpeg, Manitoba, on the unceded lands of Pimicikamak. His most recent books are *Sukun: New and Selected Poems* and the nonfiction book *Northern Light: Power, Land, and the Memory of Water*, winner of the Banff Mountain Book Competition Award for Environmental Literature. He is the author of numerous other volumes of poetry, fiction, essay, and cross-genre work. He is also a translator and editor, and currently works as a Professor of Comparative Literature and Literary Arts at the University of California, San Diego.

Typeset in Arno and Brandon Printed.

Printed at the Coach House on bpNichol Lane in Toronto, Ontario, on Zephyr Antique Laid paper, which was manufactured, acid-free, in Saint-Jérôme, Quebec, from second-growth forests. This book was printed with vegetable-based ink on a 1973 Heidelberg KORD offset litho press. Its pages were folded on a Baumfolder, gathered by hand, bound on a Sulby Auto-Minabinda, and trimmed on a Polar single-knife cutter.

Coach House is located in Toronto, which is on the traditional territory of many nations, including the Mississaugas of the Credit, the Anishnabeg, the Chippewa, the Haudenosaunee, and the Wendat peoples, and is now home to many diverse First Nations, Inuit, and Métis peoples. We acknowledge that Toronto is covered by Treaty 13 with the Mississaugas of the Credit. We are grateful to live and work on this land.

Edited by Alana Wilcox
Cover design by Crystal Sikma, cover art *The Magical Man* by Jatin Das
Interior design by Crystal Sikma
Author photo by Jesse Sutton

Coach House Books
80 bpNichol Lane
Toronto ON M5S 3J4
Canada

mail@chbooks.com
www.chbooks.com